Growing up, most people

make plans for their lives.

But even the best laid plans

can go awry. Are Sarah and

Jackie ready for all the

drama life seems to dish

out?

I would like to dedicate this book to my mom, Lynne; to my children, Caden and Kyla; and to my loving husband, David. Thank you for always being my biggest fans and always cheering me on. I love you more than words could ever say. David, you are definitely my better half! Thank you for supporting me and loving me through everything. I love you, Babe!

1

Sarah Sanders was of average height with long brown hair and bright blue eyes. She grew up in a loving home in the 1990s. It was an old farmhouse with lots of character and—without exception—very neat and welcoming. Family photos lined the staircase leading to the three bedrooms upstairs. The photos showed a very happy, closely knit family. Her home was continually filled with the enticing aroma of coffee and whatever her mom was cooking that day—usually, more than needed; always, someone around to eat it! People tended to gravitate towards their home. It just seemed to be the place to go if you needed to talk or if you were down on your luck and needed a warm meal.

Sarah's parents, Jen and Greg, were a happily married Christian couple who had a heart for others. They never wanted to see anyone go without. Greg was a handsome man with dark hair and blue eyes. At 5'7", he had become very muscular after many years of hard physical labour. Jen was 5'4" with shoulder-length blonde hair and brown eyes. She was a little on the heavy side—trying to lose weight for as long as Sarah could remember. They had met in college in the same business program.

"It was those beautiful eyes that got to me," Greg would say romantically about Jen. "It always felt as though she could see right through me."

"I found him so annoying." Jen would fake seriousness in a whisper.

Greg would always stick out his lower lip when she said this and pretend to be sad.

"But he grew on me...eventually." Her laughter would make him smile again. That story had been repeated so many times over the years that Sarah knew every word by heart. And she would roll her eyes every time. Her parents had dated for two years before getting married and having Sarah, their only child. They loved spending time together as a family.

Sarah had been a blessing to Greg and Jen. They had both decided, before they got married, that they only wanted one child. That way they could give their child all the things they never had. Greg was the second of seven children. Looking back, Greg knew that his parents had done all they could for him and his siblings, and that it had been a struggle for them to keep everyone clothed and fed. Jen had also come from a big family. She was the youngest of five sisters with an alcoholic father. Until Jen was ten years old, her life was constantly in turmoil. Her mother would often have bruises and black eyes. But then, her dad drank himself to death. It was a horrible thing to go through but she had found her house—and her life—becoming much calmer after that. A couple of years later, Jen's mom met a good Christian man who loved her siblings and her mom the way a man should. After all that Greg and Jen had

gone through growing up, they
agreed on having only one child—
it would be much easier!

Greg became a
professional carpenter and
worked for various companies
over the years. But, lately he had
become tired of the irregular
shifts and long hours—and, tired
of working for other people. Even
though he made good money,
making it possible for Jen to stay
home and care for Sarah, he
would complain to Jen that he
disliked his job.

"Oh Greg, if you feel this way, start your own business!" Jen would say.

"One day." he would always respond.

Greg was such a good carpenter that his customers at work started asking if he did any work on the side, and would request custom cupboards and tables. So he converted his garage into a workshop and started buying more and more tools. He soon found himself working harder on his days off than on an average full day at work. His little side business quickly grew too big for his workshop, as happy customers started sending their friends and family his way. At the same time, the workshop turned into a bit of a gathering place for men in the community. Greg never knew from day to day who would show up, but it wasn't very often that he was alone. He didn't mind—he would just put everyone to work while they chatted. He was a very insightful and wise man.

Eventually, Greg realized that he was running himself

ragged. After a lot of convincing on Jen's part, he finally agreed to ask the bank for a loan to buy the warehouse down the street—the perfect place to go into business on his own. Sarah—five years old at the time—could remember thinking how funny it was to see her dad dressed up in a suit and tie.

"Why are you wearing that, Daddy?" she asked him.

"Well, Honey, I'm wearing this so the bank will know that I'm a real businessman and give me a loan to buy a larger workshop," he had replied.

"But, Daddy, when you work, you're covered in sawdust. How will they *know* you're a real businessman if you're all dressed up?"

Greg and Jen had looked at each other, speechless for a second—as they often were when Sarah said something that seemed wiser than her years.

"Well, that's a really good point, Honey, but I don't think they'd like me walking in and dropping sawdust everywhere."

Sarah nodded and walked away. That had satisfied her curiosity. Greg and Jen just laughed.

"I'll be praying!!" called Jen, after Greg kissed her and Sarah goodbye.

Greg had arrived, nervously, at the bank, praying that he wouldn't sweat through his shirt. He had all the paperwork he thought he needed to convince the bank manager. He had come prepared.

Floating home that afternoon, Greg broke the

exciting news to his family: the loan had been approved!! Celebrations were in order for their new beginning!

Greg quit his job and his own business continued to expand. He and Jen were able to hire a couple men who were down on their luck and who no one else seemed to have any time for. As Greg got to know them, he discovered that they had a lot to offer. One had experience driving a truck; the other had a background in carpentry. They had lost their way due to bad decisions or just the curve balls life tends to throw at everyone at one point or another.

Bad decisions. Greg knew all about those. His own story had not always been one of success and happiness. A womanizer before he met Jen, he broke a lot of hearts, treated a lot of people badly, and acted as though everyone owed him something. When he met Jen, he had decided that he needed to change his ways. There was something about her that made him want to be different, to do

16

better. Not to say that he was instantly a new man, but Jen was very patient, and they worked together on those changes. And when they had Sarah, it made everything that much better. Now, they had been married for twenty years and he wouldn't change it for the world. He was a very blessed man!

2

Growing up, Sarah wished that she could be like the kids she saw on TV, with tons of trophies and ribbons from the great things they had accomplished. Like her mom, she struggled with her weight and she felt self-conscious about it. In grade school, kids would make fun of her and call her names. She continually felt unnoticed, faded, in the background...until they wanted to tease someone. So, Sarah was

often lonely until she met Jackie
in grade six.

Jackie had moved from the
other end of the city when her
grandmother died and her mom
inherited the house. Sarah and
Jackie quickly became like
sisters, doing everything together.
Sarah finally felt she could be
herself with someone other than
her parents. She finally had
someone her own age that cared
about her.

Jackie often spent time at
Sarah's house because, although
Jackie's mom tried, she was not

19

able to provide very much for her daughter. She was supporting her lazy boyfriend as well as Jackie and herself. The house always smelled of cigarette smoke and stale beer. Her mom's boyfriend would lie on the couch in his underwear and the only reason he would go anywhere was to get more cigarettes or beer. Her mom would leave him in charge of Jackie, but he was too lazy to do anything except yell at her. He would make himself supper but refuse to do anything for Jackie. Her supper was always whatever her mom was able to bring home from the restaurant where she worked as a waitress. But, because Jackie never knew when her mom would be home, she would often just grab cookies or something like that out of the cupboard. It really wasn't the type of home where any kid would want to be. But, whenever Jackie visited Sarah she felt like one of the family. They welcomed her into their home and loved her as one of their own. If it hadn't been for Sarah's parents, Jackie's life might not have held as much hope for her.

In Grade 7, Sarah had a huge crush on a boy named Brian. She had gone through grade school with him and had a soft spot for him ever since he let her borrow his pencil in math class. She had turned every look and every smile he gave her into something much bigger than it really was. She was convinced that he felt the same. They would talk in class and laugh at the same jokes. She thought for sure he was the one for her. Maybe their story would be like one of those romantic love stories in those corny movies! When the

22

night of the Hallowe'en dance arrived, Sarah and Jackie had both dressed up to impress the boys. Jackie was a natural beauty and Sarah envied her for that. She knew that all the boys would be delighted to dance with Jackie. But this time, Brian would be there for Sarah, and she happily, hopefully finished getting ready.

When she and Jackie walked into the dimly lit, romantically transformed gym, Sarah felt on top of the world. Even though Brian hadn't said anything to her about the dance, she knew that he would be looking forward to dancing with her. She scanned the room and finally spotted Brian. For the first time she felt confident, despite the butterflies in her stomach. She had played out the whole scene in her mind: *they would lock eyes from across the room; he would walk over to her and say, Wow! You look amazing! Nervously... cutely... he would ask her to dance, they would dance the whole night, and he would shyly admit that he had like her for a long time.* Sarah looked Brian's way several times. She crossed the floor and passed his cluster of friends, trying to attract Brian's attention, but after several unsuccessful attempts, she found Jackie and confided her discouragement. Jackie didn't miss a beat:

"I'll go ask him!" Jackie said as she started across the dance floor.

No, don't! Sarah wanted to yell in horror. But, at the same time, she really wanted to hear him say, *Yes, I'd love to.* So, instead, Sarah watched from the back corner of the gym as Jackie approached Brian. She couldn't hear what they were saying, but she clearly saw the look of confusion on Brian's face. Then, Jackie pointed over to her and his confusion turned to disgust. He was shaking his head and then, when Jackie turned back in Sarah's direction, he could be seen laughing with his friends.

Sarah was devastated. She ran out of the gym in tears.

"Wait!" Jackie called, and ran after her.

"How could I have gotten it so wrong?" asked Sarah. "I really thought he liked me! How stupid am I? Who would like a fat girl like me, anyway?"

"You're beautiful! If he can't see that, it's his problem!"

"Thanks..." But, Sarah just didn't buy it. Jackie's beautiful, she thought. I'm nothing like her.

3

Sarah became obsessed with losing weight. If I looked more like Jackie, she thought, guys like Brian would like me. She began eating a bit less at meals and being even more careful about her choice of foods. The numbers on her scale began to show weight loss–it was exciting to watch them get closer and closer to good weight. Her clothes started to fit better and she started feeling much better about herself. Sarah's mom was starting to notice, too. At first Jen thought it was good because Sarah had been so self-conscious about her weight in the past and she was now creating healthier changes. But then she began to see that this was becoming an obsession with Sarah. And, she worried that Sarah was doing it for the wrong reasons. Jen decided to register Sarah and herself at the local gym. Sarah loved the idea and she and her mom would go together every morning, spend time together, and prepare healthy meals together at home.

They were getting in shape the healthy way.

Sarah continued to work out with her mom most mornings. But after a while, she started missing some gym sessions. Something would come up and she would just cancel. Sometimes she was just too tired to go. She wished that staying in shape wasn't so hard! She saw people like Jackie who didn't even have to try to stay in shape! Jackie ate whatever she wanted and never had a weight problem. *Ugh! It's just not fair!* she would always end up thinking. Some days she would carefully follow the healthy eating plan her mom and doctor had told her about; other days she felt as though she had just eaten everything in the house! It was a constant battle with food. It seemed to be either her enemy or her best friend. As a result, she was always self-conscious. She never felt worthy of anyone's attention. When a boy showed interest in her she didn't care how he treated her, she was just thankful he wanted to be with her.

Over the next few years, Sarah had her share of strange encounters with guys. Justin was one of these. He was the brother of one of her dad's workers in the shop. She had met him when she was sixteen years old. He was eighteen. One day he showed up to drive his brother home from work and Sarah was just leaving for home herself. It was a cold winter evening and Sarah was running out to warm up her car when she noticed him sitting in a blue pickup truck in the parking lot. He noticed her, too, and got out of his truck.

"Hey!" said Justin, as Sarah crossed the parking lot.

"Hey," replied Sarah.

"I'm just waiting for my brother."

"Ah...okay, you're Kyle's brother."

"Yah, but don't hold that against me!" He flashed a flirtatious smile.

"I won't...." laughed Sarah. She was attracted to him right away. He was a little taller than her, with blonde hair and blue eyes. She was flattered that he was actually talking with her.

"I'm Justin, by the way." He held his out his hand.

"Nice to meet you, Justin. I'm Sarah." She shook his hand and noticed that he looked directly into her eyes. As soon as their hands touched, she felt a spark.

When Kyle came out of the shop, he noticed Justin and Sarah chatting. "Oh, I see you two have met!"

"Yes, we have!" they both said at the same time and laughed.

"Man, I really hope they fix my car soon so I don't have to wait for Casanova here every day after work!" Kyle rolled his eyes. Kyle was five years older than Justin and the complete opposite of him. Where Justin was witty and charming, Kyle was impatient and sarcastic.

"Well, I guess I'd better get Mr. Happy Pants home," said Justin to Sarah. "I hope I run into you again soon!"

"Me too!" Sarah felt herself blush.

The next day, Sarah went back to the shop for a couple hours after school. It was a short walking distance from home so she often met her dad there. When they were finished for the day, they headed out to the parking lot and there was Justin, sitting in his blue pickup truck.

"If you're looking for Kyle, he left about an hour ago," called Sarah, excited to see him again.

"Actually, I was hoping to see *you!* Do you want to go grab something to eat?" he asked.

"Sure! I'd love to!" She turned around and looked at her dad. "Is that okay, Dad?"

"Go ahead. Don't be late!" her father said, loud enough that Justin could hear him.

"Yessir!" Justin called back.

"Thanks, Dad!" said Sarah as she jumped into Justin's truck.

"I just need to stop at my buddy's house on the way,

okay?" asked Justin as they
headed down the street.

"Sure." Sarah felt nervous.
She didn't like meeting new
people like this. She really hoped
that he wouldn't want her to come
in with him. They drove for a few
minutes and then pulled into a
driveway not far from Sarah's
house.

"I'll be right back, okay?"
he asked

"Okay." Sarah was
relieved that she didn't have to go
in. She sat and listened to the
radio, wondering where they

might go to eat and why they needed to stop here. She waited...and waited. The time crept from 5:00pm to 5:20pm...where was he? Finally, when Sarah's watch read 5:45pm and Justin still hadn't emerged from that house, she got out of the truck and walked home. She was hungry, tired, and heart-broken.

"That was quick!" her dad called from the kitchen.

"Well, it turned out that he had other things he needed to do." Sarah hoped to avoid a million questions. In the distance, she heard her mom's voice asking her dad a question— enough of a distraction for Sarah to get away.

The next day after school she went back to the shop. When she arrived, Kyle was still there.

"Hey, Kyle," said Sarah, "what's up with your brother?! He took me out last night and left me waiting in his truck, while he went into his buddy's house! I finally just walked home!"

"Oh, he probably just went in to smoke up and lost track of

the time." Kyle was nonchalant, as if this was something that people did all the time.

"Wow! That's nice!" Sarah's sarcasm surprised even her. Justin never bothered to show his face again.

Then there was the guy who proclaimed his love to Sarah until she discovered that he was still with his girlfriend of four years!

Sarah spent lots of time and money on guys who didn't appreciate her; Jen spent many hours trying to figure out how to get through to her. Jen prayed that Sarah would see her own worth; Greg would just tell Jen that Sarah would have to figure it out for herself, and then secretly pray for Sarah himself.

When she was seventeen, Sarah met Tom Brown in high school. His dark brown hair and blue eyes charmed her in biology class. He was a lot taller than her and a big fan of Bon Jovi and Collective Soul and had band stickers all over his binders. She had noticed him around school joking with his friends and smoking outside. She was always falling for the "bad guys", assuming that they would change if she was with them—that she could somehow save them. Though her past relationships had proven otherwise, Sarah remained a hopeless romantic.

Sarah and Tom got to know each other over the body of a dead frog that stunk of formaldehyde. As they dissected, they talked, and Sarah found herself hanging onto his every word. She didn't want to admit it, but she was falling for him.

Sometimes after school Sarah and Jackie would meet at the town coffee shop where all the high school kids hung out. The tall dividers between the booths gave them privacy to talk about anything. They would pretend to study for whatever big test was coming up, but mostly they would talk about their latest crush and who was dating who. When Tom entered Sarah's life, his name came up more and more in her conversations with Jackie. Jackie quickly realized that there was something going on between Sarah and Tom.

"Really, Sarah?! Why are you giving that jerk the time of day? Didn't you hear what he did to his last girlfriend...uh-h...Joanna Turner? He cheated on her with Jenny Ryan, the most popular girl in school. When Jenny wanted nothing more to do with him, he went crawling back to Joanna! The worst part is: Joanna actually took him back and he stayed 'til he got bored and cheated again with some other girl at another school."

But Sarah couldn't help it. She had that all-too-familiar gut feeling that Jackie was right and

she should just forget about Tom,

but the more Jackie protested,

the more she felt she had to show

Jackie that he really was a great

guy.

Sarah found herself

spending a little extra time getting

ready every morning and being

very disappointed on the days

Tom wasn't at school. Jackie's

warnings about him still made her

feel uneasy at times, but she

would just ignore them and tell

herself that people can change.

4

Tom Brown was eighteen.
He had grown up in Niagara Falls
with his mom and dad, Jim and
Carole. Jim Brown worked for the
hydro company. He was a very
harsh man. Carole was beautiful,
tall and thin with dark brown hair
and green eyes. Unfortunately,
she was a push-over and did
everything that Jim wanted her to
do. Her whole worth was based
on what kind of mood Jim was in
when he got home. He loved to
spend his weekends at the bar

drinking and hooking up with whatever women he met.

Even though he wasn't much to look at with his thinning hair and beer belly, he was a smooth talker and able to make women fall all over themselves for him. Carole had known this about him for years. Friends used to call telling her they had seen him with another woman and ask her why she wouldn't leave him. *I'm not going anywhere*, she would say. Eventually, they stopped calling.

It was a very lonely existence for Carole. She would

spend most of her days cleaning up from Jim's night-before. On many nights he would come home drunk, stumbling and breaking whatever lay in his path. He would stagger sideways into walls and leave his imprint, fall onto the coffee table, and then get sick wherever he was in the room. Try as she might, Carole could never get rid of that smell. Her whole existence was damage control. She tried hard to be a better example for their son, Tom, but always felt that she fell short because she could never find the courage to leave Jim. She had

wanted to leave many times—had
even packed a bag for herself
and Tom once, when Jim was
out, but she had backed out at
the last minute. She had nowhere
to go. Jim would remind her when
she forgot how wonderful he was.
He would tell her how she had
nothing without him.

Jim hadn't always been
this way. When he and Carole
were first together, life was good.
He treated her like gold and
promised her the world. Then,
once they were married, things
changed. He became short-

tempered and started drinking more. Carole thought maybe a baby would make things better. She begged him for a baby. He wanted nothing to do with the idea. When Carole discovered that she was pregnant, Jim blamed her and wouldn't talk to her for a week. Eventually he came around to the idea, when Carole convinced him that he wouldn't have to care for the baby at all.

"I don't want that thing keeping me up all night," he would say.

Carole didn't recognize this man anymore. Was this going to be her life from now on?

After Tom was born, Jim realized that women really loved a guy with a baby and he would take Tom out every chance he got. Carole would get angry when Jim would bring little Tom home with lipstick all over his head. But she didn't want to fight, so she just washed it off—sometimes with her own tears.

As Tom got older, he had a large group of friends and he had his pick of the girls. They loved his blue eyes, brown hair, tall stature. He had his father's charm and his mother's good looks, and he knew what to say to seduce them. But then he began hearing that he was getting a bad reputation with them. He didn't really understand why drama followed him so much. Why did Joanna get so mad at him when he hooked up with Jenny? It's not like they were married. He had a right to do whatever he wanted, didn't he? He had made his mistakes, but it was only because of everyone else.

Tom and his friends would sometimes meet up at the coffee shop after school. They would sit in the smoking room and goof off, making fun of each other and talking about sports, music, and girls.

It was on one of those coffee-shop afternoons that Tom noticed Sarah sitting with a friend...Jenny? Was it really Jenny?! Oh, who cares, he thought. Wasn't Sarah in his class? Why was she so nice to him—she must have heard about him, right? Most of the girls at school now wouldn't even look at him anymore, but maybe Sarah would understand that he did those things because of the way *they* treated *him*. Maybe she would see that it wasn't *his* fault at all. Why did they always think he needed to be controlled, that *he* needed to change?

Tom would brag that he was going to grow up to be just like his old man and, unfortunately, that was beginning to be the case. Jim had convinced Tom at a young age that women were inferior to men and were only on this earth to meet whatever needs men might have at the time. Tom had grown up with this chip on his shoulder, as if he had been taught a secret that no one else knew. He had tried to enlighten his best friend, Robbie, but Robbie had said that he was a Christian and that he respected women and something about them being equal. He always zoned out when Robbie started talking like that. Robbie had even tried to get him to come to church for some youth group, but he had squashed that with, *that stuff's for you, not for me!*

Tom and Robbie had been friends since grade 7. They had met in art class and bonded over the same music styles. Now that they were getting older, Robbie was getting more serious about his life and his future. Tom, however, was still the same party guy that Robbie had met all those years ago. Tom wasn't sure what he wanted for his future and just spent his weekdays showing up at school, then smoking and drinking coffee with the guys. On the weekends, it was more than coffee.

Robbie had noticed Tom talking about Sarah Sanders. He was hoping this would be different than Tom's previous relationships—he hadn't treated them very well. Robbie had heard that Sarah was a Christian and had tried to talk Tom out getting involved with her by saying that she would want him to go to church and that she would want him to change. Tom just said that he didn't care, that she couldn't make him do anything he didn't want to. Since his mother had never disobeyed his father, he didn't see this as an issue, as long as Sarah knew what her role was to be in the relationship.

Tom liked talking to Sarah because he could tell that she was his type of girl. She wouldn't expect a lot from him and—most importantly—she would do anything for him. Her face always lit up when she saw him, and he often saw her scanning the crowded halls for him at school. This was going to work out really well, he thought.

5

Jackie Templeton had been best friends with Sarah for as long as she could remember. They were like sisters. Jackie loved hanging out with Sarah but would get exasperated by her choice in boys sometimes. She always deserved so much better, but sold herself short.

Jackie, on the other hand, would never let any boy treat her like garbage. She was beautiful—tall, thin, blonde with brown eyes—and very driven. She knew that she wanted to become a successful business woman like her Aunt Jane in Vancouver. She wanted to work in one of those tall office buildings and wear power suits. Nothing was going to get in her way.

Jackie had seen John Simmons around school since grade 9 but never really talked to him until they were in the same English class in grade 10. He liked her right away. He asked her out, but she was apprehensive. He was so sweet and caring that she could only resist him for so long. The second time he asked her out, she said yes. They had been dating for just over a year and they were the envy of many of their high school classmates. John knew when Jackie needed space to study or to hang out with Sarah and he respected that. He loved her and felt so blessed to have found a girl like her. She motivated him to be diligent with his school work and to think about his future. *I'm not going to support any man*, she would say. That made him sit up and take notice. There was no way he wanted to lose her.

Jackie had grown up with a single mother. She had watched her mom date one loser after another. She would often come home from school to find a guy sitting on her couch and couldn't understand what her mother saw in any of them. Her mom worked very hard as a waitress at a local restaurant. As Jackie got older, her mother would take on more and more work hours to try to make ends meet. All the while her latest boyfriend would be at their house eating their food and sitting on their couch. Then, when they ultimately left her for some other sucker with more money, she would be devastated. Jackie was so sick of picking up the pieces. Her father had been the first in a long line of users and losers that her mother had hooked up with over the years.

Jackie promised herself at a young age that she would never support a man while he sat on her couch and she worked. When she first met John she knew right away that he was a great guy. She still found herself testing him, but each time he passed with flying colours. She loved him and could see them getting married after she had started her career as a business woman. He wanted to get into construction, building affordable housing for people in need. Jackie loved his heart for others and the passion he had for the future and, of course, for her.

Jackie spent a lot of time at Sarah's house when they were growing up. It was so nice to sit down at the dinner table and be surrounded by a family that really loved each other. Every evening before dinner they would all say grace before they ate. Jackie had not grown up in a Christian home and had never seen this practice before. It was so refreshing to see a family with real values. When things got serious with John, she introduced him to Sarah's parents before her own mother.

Jackie didn't ask a lot of questions about the Christian faith, she just knew that Sarah's home was warm and welcoming. Her own mother loved her and tried to make their home comfortable, but it just wasn't the same as Sarah's. After John had met Sarah's family, he and Jackie both decided that that's what they wanted their future home and family to be like—once they were set in their careers, of course. John's family loved Jackie and knew that she was good for their son. They often invited her to their home and would ask John how Jackie was doing if she had not visited for a while. That girl was definitely going places, they would say.

Then one morning, Jackie called John in a panic: she was late!

6

John Simmons loved life. He would wake up every morning amazed at his good fortune. He had a beautiful driven girlfriend and he was super-excited about the future. He was starting an internship with a building company that built affordable houses for people in need. When he was younger, his family fell on some hard times. Looking back he would remember how his dad, Eric, lost his job and his mom,

Amanda, worked as much as she could to make ends meet. But, Amanda was then diagnosed with multiple sclerosis and that changed everything. The fatigue and attacks she suffered made it impossible for her to work anymore. She started collecting disability but it just wasn't enough. Eric had searched everywhere for work to try to support his family. Finally, he learned of an opening for a superintendent at an apartment building. They could live rent-free while taking care of the building. Since his dad had a background in construction, this seemed ideal.It was there that John saw what real need looked like, as there were so many elderly tenants and single moms living in this deplorable apartment building. Eric spent many hours trying to fix up each of the forty apartments in the building. From neglected plumbing and electrical repairs to paint peeling off the walls, he had his hands full. The only problem was that the landlord did not like to part with his money, so Eric would often pay for the repairs himself—it broke his heart to see people living in such dreadful conditions.

Eric trained John to help with any repair that was needed. As John got older, he and his dad decided to start a business building affordable housing for those in need. Not having to pay rent for their apartment for a few years had enabled them to put some money away. When the time was right, Eric took the plunge and—with the help of some government grants—bought some old buildings and renovated them into beautiful, affordable homes. As soon as Eric's own landlord saw the success he was having, the landlord raised his rent. Without a moment's hesitation, Eric simply bought out the landlord to become the owner of his own apartment building. As he had done with previous buildings, he fixed up the apartments and rented them all at reasonable, livable rates.

Life was good for John. He had a clear view of his future

with Jackie and it seemed really bright. That was until that Monday when he got the frantic call from Jackie. She was so upset that he could barely understand what she was saying at first. When he finally calmed her down he couldn't believe what he was hearing.

"What?! How is this possible? We were so careful, Jackie."

"Well, I guess not careful enough, John!"

John's head was spinning. He couldn't breathe. How would he tell his parents? *Why did this have to happen now—we're so young!*

"Jackie, have you taken a pregnancy test?"

"Not yet."

'Then we need to get a test so we can be sure. Maybe we're freaking out for no reason!"

7

Sarah and Tom were talking more and more in class. He was so charming and sweet that she just couldn't get enough. She also felt bad for him because not many other people would talk to him anymore. To be honest, Sarah just couldn't believe that someone like Tom—tall and handsome—would even give her the time of day. She loved the attention she was getting from him. They would talk outside of class and smile at each other in the hallways. Sarah was on cloud nine but she tried to keep it to herself because she already knew Jackie's opinion—and she also knew that her own parents would not approve. Well, they just weren't as open-minded as she was.

One day in school, just after first period, Tom was waiting for her at her locker. He had never done this before. Her heart was racing! *What could he want to talk to me about?* He had a huge smile on his face that melted her heart. She knew she would say yes to almost anything just to see that smile.

"Hey, Sarah," he said. "I was wondering what you're doing after school today?"

"Nothing," she replied, even though she knew that Jackie had asked her to meet her at the coffee shop after school— something really important had come up. *Jackie will understand. I'll call her tonight.*

"Do you want to get a coffee with me?"

"Yes, I'd love to!" Sarah hadn't wanted to sound quite that excited. Tom had asked her out!

Tom met Sarah at her locker after school. His dad had let him borrow the car so that Tom could drive to the coffee shop.

"That's perfect," she said, all the while telling herself, *Don't be awkward! Just be cool. It's only coffee...COFFEE WITH TOM!!* Her palms started to sweat as she got into his bright red 1967 mustang. "Nice car," she managed to blurt out.

"Thanks. It's my dad's baby. He doesn't even let my mom drive it. But he trusts me, so that's cool."

As they were driving, Tom lit a cigarette. The smell made Sarah feel sick, but she didn't dare say anything -she might upset him! She was hoping that if he had a smoke now, maybe they wouldn't need to sit in the stuffy smoking section at the coffee shop. When they arrived they ordered their coffees and Tom reached for his wallet.

"Oh, man!" he said, "I must have forgotten my wallet at home today!"

"It's okay. I've got this." And, Sarah paid.

"Thanks, Beautiful." He led the way to the smoking section.

I guess I carry the coffees, too, she thought, as she followed him, carrying both coffees to the dreaded smoking section.

They sat and talked for a while. It was mostly Tom talking about himself and his interests. Sarah sat there trying control her feelings of nausea from the smoke and being amazed that Tom wanted to talk to her! *Yes, he seems a bit full of himself,* she thought, *but maybe he's just nervous like I am. First dates are always awkward.*

She looked at her watch and realized it was already five o'clock. Her parents would be wondering where she was.

"Tom," she said interrupting him. "It's already five o'clock. I need to get home. Sorry to cut this short, but my parents are going to kill me!"

"No prob, Babe. I see what's more important to you."

"What? No, it's not that. It's just that they worry about me."

"Yep! That's okay, Sarah. I guess we'll go then."

Sarah felt bad but she knew she had no choice—she had to go home and face the music. Right away! Plus, she had to call Jackie who would be wondering why she hadn't called to let her know that she couldn't meet her.

As they left the coffee shop, Sarah headed toward the

car with Tom. At the car, he turned to her and said, "Oh, sorry. I'm not going back your way. You don't mind walking home, do you?" It was getting dark and the coffee shop was a good twenty-minute walk to her home.

"N-No. No, of course not." She wanted to say, *Come on, Tom, you won't drive five minutes out of your way to take me home?* But she didn't want to upset him, so she added, "Thanks, Tom, this was nice." She didn't know what she was thanking him for.

"Yup, see you tomorrow."

And he was gone.

By the time Sarah got home, supper was on the table and her mom had that worried-sick look on her face.

"Sarah! Where have you been?"

"I just went for coffee with a friend and lost track of time, Mom. Sorry, I didn't call."

"What friend?"

"Tom. You don't know him. Mom, do you mind if I—quick—run upstairs and phone Jackie?"

"After supper, Honey."

"Please don't do that again without calling us." her dad added.

"Sorry, Dad. I won't."

After dinner, Sarah finally called Jackie. She couldn't wait to tell Jackie about her date—or whatever that was—with Tom. On second thought, maybe she would keep it to herself until their next date. *The next date will be better*, she thought. *But...maybe he won't ask me out again! Man, I should have let him decide when it was time to go! If I get another chance with him, I'll know better. .*

When Jackie told Sarah about her concerns, Sarah couldn't believe what she was hearing! What were Jackie and John going to do?

That night, Sarah lay awake in her bed. There was so much on her mind. She wondered about Jackie and John. She replayed her date with Tom and all the feelings it had created. She felt excited that he had asked her out, but disappointed with some of the things he had said and done. She did her best to ignore the disappointment so that the fairy tale in her mind didn't need to end.

When Tom got home from his date with Sarah, his dad was yelling at his mom. That was nothing new. *She must have done something stupid again*, he thought. *Probably didn't make the supper Dad wanted or didn't fold his laundry right. It's good that he takes the time to correct her.* He passed his parents and headed upstairs to call Robbie.

"Hey, Rob! Had a date with Sarah this aft!"

Oh no, thought Robbie, *what was this girl thinking?!* "How'd it go," he asked.

"Oh, pretty well, I think. She seems like someone who would do an okay job looking after me."

Robbie's heart sank. Tom was going to use this girl just like all the others. Robbie just prayed that Sarah wouldn't fall for it.

When Tom showed up at school the next day, he saw

Sarah. She was looking for him...
as usual. When she finally saw
him, her face lit up...as usual.
*Awesome! She really is where I
want her to be. I can treat her any
way I want and she will still be
falling over herself to make me
happy!*

8

Robbie James had grown up in a Christian home with his parents, Sue and Robert, and his younger brother, Steve. Sue was average height with bright red hair, blue eyes and fair skin. Robert was slightly taller than his wife with dark brown hair and brown eyes. Steve was the spitting image of his father while Robbie had inherited the red hair, blue eyes and fair skin from his mom. Robbie took some teasing about his red hair, but his mom would reassure him that he was very handsome.

Robbie's family, values, and morals meant a lot to him. They all enjoyed Sunday morning church and lunch at Arby's restaurant after the service. His family had witnessed big miracles in their lives and could not attribute them to anyone but the Almighty. When Sue was pregnant with Steve, the doctor ordered a routine twenty-week ultrasound. It revealed that Steve's brain was not developing properly. The doctors told Steve's parents that he would likely never breathe on his own—that he would be born in a vegetative state relying on machines to keep him alive. They advised aborting this pregnancy and trying for another baby in about a year. Robert and Sue didn't believe in abortion but also didn't want to see their baby suffer. They spent the next week after the terrible news praying for a miracle and for guidance. They went to their Tuesday night Bible study and all their friends laid hands on Sue and prayed for the baby. Steve's mom and dad felt that God was telling them to trust

Him with this pregnancy. So,

against their doctors'

recommendations, Sue carried

Steve to term. The doctors told

them that the minute Sue would

give birth, Steve would have to be

taken for testing to see if he

would ever be able to function on

his own. When Steve was born,

the doctors were amazed to hear

him let out a huge scream—as if to

let them know for certain that they

were wrong. And they were!

Testing revealed a perfectly

normal brain! Sue and Robert

called all their friends who had

been praying for them since

hearing the news so many months ago. God had performed a miracle for their perfect little baby boy! They all had celebrated in the hospital room that day! Steve was now eleven years old, progressing just like any other eleven year old!

Robbie's mom and dad were both school teachers. His mom taught grade 4 and his dad taught high school English. They always expected Robbie and Steve to keep up with their studies and get good grades. This was easy for Robbie but a little harder for Steve. They would always take time to help Steve with his homework and guide him through his challenges.

Robbie had been friends with Tom for a long time. Their friendship had been a bone of contention with Robbie's mom. She knew that the way Tom acted was not all his fault–parenting was definitely partially to blame– but Tom would come to visit and help himself to whatever was in the refrigerator without asking. He wasn't a very respectful boy. He was nothing like his mother.

Carole was a sweet, soft-spoken lady. But when Robbie would go over to Tom's house, he would come home troubled by the way Tom's father yelled and swore at Tom's mom. After Robbie's mother heard that, she imposed a strict rule that Robbie could only hang out with Tom at the James's home. She had hoped that some of their values would rub off on Tom. Robbie had always liked hanging out with Tom, although lately he had been finding it harder and harder to listen to him talk about himself all the time. He couldn't even remember the last time he got a word in edgewise. Not to mention the fact that Tom only called when he needed something or wanted to brag. Now Tom was talking about Sarah Sanders again. Tom had said that he was planning on taking her out again soon, and joked that this time he could get her to buy him dinner. But, Robbie had told him that that wasn't a joke. What Robbie didn't say was that–sadly–Sarah probably would.

Robbie had noticed Sarah in the hallways at school, too. He

had wanted to ask her out before Tom said anything about her, but he always lost his nerve. She was beautiful, and he could tell by her mannerisms that she was self-conscious. He wished she could see how beautiful she really was. Tom would never build her up. He would only use her. Robbie wished he had spoken up before Tom had claimed her, but—then again—she probably never would have noticed Robbie. He was short and a little stocky with <u>red</u> hair and fair skin. He was not the tall, dark, and handsome type like Tom. That first time that Tom brought Sarah into the coffee shop to hang out with him and Robbie, Robbie finally had a chance to talk with her and fell for her even more. They had so much more in common than she would ever have with Tom, but she just worshipped the ground Tom walked on. Robbie could see the sparkle in Sarah's eyes every time she looked at Tom. It made him feel sick watching the way Tom treated her and knowing that there was absolutely nothing he could do about it.

9

Jackie and John met up at
the coffee shop that Monday
morning. They couldn't go to
each other's homes because they
were supposed to be at school.
They sat in their usual booth
drinking their usual coffee, but
nothing was usual about today. If
Jackie was pregnant, nothing
would ever be the same again.

"You know that no matter
what, I'll support you, Jackie. I'm
not going anywhere!"

Jackie was terrified that a baby would change everything. A baby would ruin everything. What was she thinking?! Why hadn't she been more careful? Why did she even get involved with John in the first place? She loved him but she had let her heart lead, like her mother always did. She had promised herself that she wouldn't let anything get in the way of her career. Now, she might have the biggest distraction of all–a baby!!

They went to the drug store and discreetly bought a

pregnancy test, but, the

instructions said she would have

to wait until the next morning.

She needed some space to figure

things out. Everything was

happening too fast. So Jackie

promised John that she'd let him

know the results the next

morning. John—the understanding

person that he was—respected

Jackie's wishes and they each

went their own ways until then.

Jackie had so many

thoughts rushing through her

mind. *What about school? How

am I going to go through*

pregnancy in high school? I won't
even fit at my desk! There will be
so many people disappointed in
me! What will my mom say?
What will Sarah's parents say?
Then there're John's parents!
What about my future! Jackie
was starting to hyperventilate.
Okay, calm down. We don't know
anything for sure yet.

Jackie wanted, needed, to
talk with her best friend. She had
called Sarah earlier that morning,
before school. Sarah should have
been home. They often called
each other before school to talk

about what they were going to wear that day, but lately Sarah had been distracted. Jackie could tell that it was because of this relationship with Tom, and she worried about that. She really needed her best friend, especially today! Where was she?! This was a crisis! At that moment, Jackie would have given anything to have her biggest concern be what she was going to wear that day!

That night Sarah finally called. "What's up? How come you weren't at school today? I would have called you sooner and met up with you but I–"

"I think I might be pregnant!" Jackie blurted out.

"What?! How?! I mean... I know how, but when?" Sarah was completely confused.

"About a month ago, I think. Sarah, I'm freaking out! I'm not ready for all of this! What am I going to do?" Jackie was shaking.

"What did John say?"

"He says he will support me in whatever I decide."

"What do you mean 'whatever I decide'?" Sarah asked apprehensively.

"Well, if I keep it or not...if there really is anything to keep! I can't even take the test 'til the morning!"

"You're not really thinking there's a chance you might *not* keep it, are you?"

"I'm only sixteen, Sarah! What kind of mother would I be at this age?!"

"Well, I would help you and I'm sure your mother would help

out, and my parents see you as a second daughter so they would love to help you, too. You will have lots of support, Jackie."

Jackie and Sarah spent the next two hours talking about all the different possibilities. If Jackie really was pregnant what would that look like? How would that change everything?

"We don't know anything about being pregnant except that you get fat!" cried Jackie. "I don't know how to change diapers or feed babies!"

Sarah tried to reassure her that no one really knows everything beforehand. "We will have our moms to talk to and hopefully John's mom will be cool and help you out, too."

"I just don't know if I can do this, Sarah!" Jackie's voice suddenly dropped to a whisper. Jackie broke into tears, and then so did Sarah.

"Do you want me to be there when you take the test?" Sarah asked. "I'll just tell my parents that I'm leaving early to help you with something before school."

"Yes...please...Mom...w-will be at work," she said between sobs.

Sarah got up early the next morning and hurried over to Jackie's. They carefully followed each step of the test then waited the longest two minutes of their teenage lives.

"You look at it, Sarah," pleaded Jackie.

Sarah picked up the test stick then looked, wide-eyed, at Jackie—it was positive!

"How will you tell him?" asked Sarah.

"I don't know. I guess I'll wait until when we meet at the coffee shop today." Jackie felt her emotions draining away. "Thanks so much for being here with me. Sarah. You need to get to school now."

"Let me know how it goes! I love you!"

"I will," Jackie replied, "I love you, too." Then Sarah was gone, and it was time for Jackie to make the unbelievably hard phone call to John.

10

John tossed and turned all night. He couldn't get his mind to stop racing. How could he have been so careless? He really loved Jackie and had been planning their future in his mind for months. Having a baby at sixteen years old was not a part of it! *That's okay, though*, he thought. *I'll just work more with Dad and save up as much money as I can. Jackie and I will have to get married soon, too. But will our parents go for that? ...We'll just have to cross that bridge when we come to it. We still don't even know if it's true yet, anyway. Maybe all this worry is for nothing!* With that thought, he was able to lull himself to sleep for an hour or so.

The next morning, John anxiously waited for the phone to ring. He longed to hear Jackie on the other end saying this was all a false alarm. Finally, she called.

"Hey," she said, "can we meet at the coffee shop? I don't want to talk about this here in case our parents overhear us."

"Of course," now John was really getting nervous! This must be serious! But it can't be true—John willed it to not be true.

When they met at the coffee shop, Jackie confirmed his fears. They were going to have a baby! They sat in silent disbelief for what seemed like forever. Then Jackie broke the silence.

"I talked with Sarah last night. She says that we will have lots of support…if we keep it."

"Well, what else would we do?" John felt a bit wary.

"I can't fathom abortion, but I was thinking about adoption," she replied.

"You could really give our baby away?!"

"Well, I just don't know how well we could support a baby, John. We're only sixteen."

"I'll work with my dad and save money for us..."

"I don't know, John. But at least we have a few months to decide."

A few days later, Jackie went to the doctor who confirmed

without a doubt that she was approximately four weeks along. The time had come to tell their parents. They started with John's. At first they were in shock. They couldn't believe that both John *and* Jackie could have been so careless. John's mom blamed herself. She had often felt that her multiple sclerosis had taken away her ability to be a good, involved mother and that this confirmed it. If she hadn't been so tired all the time, if she had spent more time with John and asked more questions about where he and Jackie were going all the time, maybe this wouldn't have happened. She also started blaming Jackie. The girl who they had thought was such a great influence for John suddenly had become the enemy, the bad influence. Her son would never have made those choices if he hadn't come under her influence.

John's father got lost in his work as he had done so often in the past during stressful situations. *I thought we taught him better than that*, he thought to himself as he smashed a hammer into a wall that he was knocking down on one of his new properties. *Didn't we show him how hard life is when you are an adult—never mind being a kid trying to raise a kid!*

Next they told Jackie's mom. She was shocked but, at the same time, was excited at the prospect of being a grandma. She was going to do her best to help them out. Maybe she would even kick out the last loser who had moved in with them.

Eventually John's parents came around to the reality of the pregnancy. As Jackie's belly grew, so did their excitement to meet their first grandchild. John's mother kept her feelings about Jackie to herself, deciding it was better to keep the enemy close. She also knew that she would love that grandchild. None of this was the baby's fault.

School was definitely interesting for John and Jackie. Especially as the months went on and they could no longer hide the fact that she was pregnant. Between John's parents and her mother, Jackie was well cared for. All her needs were met, from maternity clothes to her odd food cravings. John was really thankful for how helpful everyone had been. Even Sarah's parents had chipped in and assured them that everything would be okay. John began to believe that they were going to make it after all.

11

Sarah and Tom had gone out pretty consistently since their first date at the coffee shop. She still felt so amazed that Tom was interested in her. She tried to overlook the fact that he always seemed to need her to pay, or to be the one to drive so he could just sit and relax. She just didn't think she could do any better. There were certain times that Tom would look at her and Sarah would melt. She would remember in those moments what she saw in him. There was something about him that made her feel special. He needed her. She loved that feeling. She would look past the fact that her parents didn't like Tom. Even when she talked with Jackie, she had started to hide details of things that Tom would do or say. But that was okay because no one really understood him like she did.

Sarah spent as much time as she could with Jackie. It was hard to believe that she was having a baby at her age! But

Sarah also had to watch the time because Tom never understood why she would need to be out with anyone other than him for longer than an hour or two. Sarah understood that he missed her when he didn't know what she was doing, so she always tried to make sure he was okay with her plans. If she didn't check with him first, she would spend the rest of the day trying to explain why she had been gone so long. It just wasn't worth it.

One day, Tom and Sarah went to the coffee shop to meet

up with his best friend, Robbie.
Sarah had seen him around
school but had never talked to
him before. He was a great guy—
Christian, too. It made her feel
really good that Tom had a friend
like him. She took it as proof that
there was more good in Tom than
met the eye. Robbie, Sarah and
Tom talked and laughed the
whole time they were together.
Sarah felt so happy to be able to
hang out as a couple with
someone else and just have a
great time. She hadn't noticed
Tom gradually becoming quieter
until they were about to leave.

"What's wrong, Tom?"

"Nothing."

Oh, here we go! I must have done something wrong again, Sarah thought. "Listen," she said. "I'm sorry if I did something wrong. I thought we had a good time, didn't we?"

Tom didn't say anything until they got into the car. "Everything was fine until you started staring at the guy at the next table!"

"What guy?!" asked Sarah.

"The guy at the next table! Don't tell me you didn't stare at him, because I know you did!" Tom's anger filled the car. "That was so disrespectful, Sarah, and now you're going to lie about it?!"

Sarah was devastated. She thought it had been a great night. Now she was wracking her brain to figure out when she could have been looking at a guy at the next table. She hadn't even noticed anyone there! Why didn't Tom realize that she only had eyes for him? From that night on, she knew she had to be careful where she looked when she was with Tom. She never wanted him to feel disrespected. After all, it was an honor to be going out with him. The other day he had even called her his girlfriend.

12

Robbie hadn't talked to Tom since they were at the coffee shop with Sarah. To be honest, he had been dodging Tom. It was too hard seeing him and Sarah together and hearing how he talked to her—like he was ordering her around. Robbie didn't understand what she saw in him.

Robbie had seen Sarah's friend, Jackie, around school. She was getting quite big. *How difficult that must be!* He had never imagined he would see one of his classmates pregnant in high school. He said a prayer for her and John. He also prayed for Sarah to see the light and dump Tom. Unfortunately, that prayer wouldn't be answered for a long time.

Robbie had been spending a lot of time thinking about what he wanted to do with his life after high school. He really liked working with kids, and often helped in the Sunday School at his church. After a lot of thought and prayer, he decided that he would like to become a youth pastor. When he told his parents, they were thrilled. He looked into Bible colleges and found one that sounded like a good choice and that was only about an hour from home. *Perfect! I can live at home and still attend my own church on Sundays*.

Robbie and Sarah began chatting more often when they saw each other in the halls at school. Maybe becoming a youth pastor would be something he and Sarah could talk about the next time he saw her. He just couldn't get her off his mind.

Even though he was trying to stay focused on his plans, she was on his mind. He didn't like seeing her with Tom. There used to be a sparkle in her eyes. Now that sparkle was gone. Whenever he saw them together, he wanted to grab her hand and pull her away from him, but he just settled for their short conversations in the hallway. Maybe someday she would see that Tom didn't really love her and that he did.

13

Jackie's life as a pregnant teenager was filled with challenges. As the months crept by, she became more and more uncomfortable. Her conversations with Sarah had turned from talking about boys or what they would wear the next day, to: "I wonder if it's a boy or a girl?" or "I wonder what will *fit* me tomorrow?!" Some of her classmates who used to talk with her now avoided her as if she were contagious. She would watch in envy when the other students were checking out colleges and she was checking out cribs and strollers. This was not what she had planned.

The bigger her belly grew, the more Jackie resented this baby and John. Even though John was extremely supportive and he loved her like crazy, she couldn't help being angry.

As Jackie's due date drew closer, John noticed that Jackie was becoming more and more distant. He tried to keep her spirits up and reassured her that all was going to be okay, but she just seemed to be in her own little world most of the time.

It was decided that Jackie and John would live with John's parents, sharing John's room. And there would be plenty of space there for a bassinet and crib. Jackie's mom, John's mom and Sarah threw a baby shower which provided everything the baby would need. They were all ready for the arrival.

14

Sarah and Tom had been going out for four months now. She had brought him home to meet her parents on a couple occasions. Greg and Jen were not crazy about him.

"Stop settling for these guys, Sarah!" her mom would say.

Sarah was insulted when her mom would say things like that. How could she consider the only guy that loved Sarah to be just like all the others?!

Some days were easier than others. Sarah began to read Tom's moods and knew when it was okay for her to speak up and when it wasn't. Sometimes she would cancel plans she had made or would just stop making plans all together. She felt really guilty when she cancelled on Jackie or her mom. She just didn't want Tom to be upset. It was easy for her mom and Jackie to say things like: "Oh, come on, Sarah. You can live without him for one night!" But deep down she was afraid that he would leave her. Once in a while, he would threaten to leave her when she did something really out of line, like not calling him as soon as she got home from school. *He loves me so much that he can't stand missing me,* she would tell herself. *It's sweet...in a weird way.*

Being a Christian, Sarah always knew she wanted to wait until she was married. But sleeping with Tom was another thing that he had pushed her to do. He would tell her that if she real-l-l-ly loved him she would. She tried to stand up for what she believed in but she couldn't imagine life without Tom. He would tell her that it was okay because they were going to be together forever. Somehow that made it easier to justify everything in her mind. So she gave in, and this became another on her list of duties that he expected her to perform for him.

Sarah began to feel that her happiness depended solely on whether Tom was happy or not. She didn't know how to have her own feelings anymore.

Between work, school, and Tom,

there was no time left for herself.

It was becoming much more

difficult to focus on school work

and, at work, she was making

mistakes. When she wasn't at

work, Tom took up all her time.

He didn't care that she was tired.

In fact, when she said that she

was tired, all he would do was

question why. So, to make life

easier she just stopped saying it.

15

Tom was happy with the way things were going with Sarah. What was there *not* to be happy about? She did everything for him! She even worked and paid for their dates and gave him money when he was short! Plus, she worked every weekend so that gave him the chance to live the single life. He could hook up with whoever he wanted to and she wouldn't know. He knew she wouldn't dare ask, even if she suspected something. It really was the perfect set up.

Tom's dad had always told him to look out for number one. Never let a woman play the equal rights card. When Tom finally brought Sarah over to meet his parents, his father could tell she was meeting the criteria and his mother wept when no one could hear her. She wept for the poor girl that was destined to live a life that was empty and loveless if she stayed with Tom. She would have to find a way to get her alone and warn her.

The opportunity finally presented itself one night a couple weeks later when Sarah came over for dinner. When dinner was finished and Sarah asked if she could help with the dishes, his mom jumped at the chance.

"Yes, I'd love some help, Sarah." And, when the guys went into the living room, Carole continued. "Sarah, you are such a beautiful girl! Let me first say that I love my son but he will only drag you down!"

Sarah couldn't believe what she was hearing. How could his own mother say this? Maybe everyone's warnings from the beginning had been right. Maybe he really was as bad for her as they had said. No, she couldn't believe that.

"No, I think you're wrong, Mrs. Brown. I know he had a bad reputation before, but he's changed since then. I'm amazed you can't see it."

"Sarah, Honey, I know you really care about Tom and you want to see the best, but it's not

144

there. He's not good for you. He's too much like his father. I don't want to see you having to live the way I do—always having to second guess yourself..."

Sarah could feel her cheeks burning with anger. How could his mother say something like about her own son?

Just then, Tom walked into the kitchen. "Ready to go, Babe?"

"Yup, let's go," said Sarah. "Thanks for supper, Mrs. Brown. Have a great night." Sarah hurried out of the kitchen, still angry at what she had heard.

Thankfully, Tom didn't even notice that she was upset so she didn't have to explain. All he cared about was going for a drive and getting her into the back seat of the car.

That night when Tom dropped her off, he went home and set up his next date with another girl– during Sarah's next work shift. If he played his cards right, he could even convince Sarah to lend him money to pay for it. Like she had before.

16

John was working hard these days to put money away for his family. He daydreamed about what it was going to be like to hold his baby girl or boy. A girl or boy—it didn't matter to him as long as the baby was healthy. He loved feeling the baby kick in Jackie's belly. He couldn't believe that that was his child in there. *What a blessing! I hope the baby looks like Jackie,* he thought.

One Monday night, John and Jackie decided to get out of the house and go to the coffee shop. It was two days before her due date. They sat at a table—Jackie couldn't fit into their usual booth anymore. As they were talking, Jackie felt a very strong pain in her abdomen. For a moment, it took her breath away.

"Are you okay, Jackie?" John asked with concern in his eyes. "Is it the baby?"

"Yes, I think I'm okay. I've been having these pains off and on since last week. I saw the

148

doctor and he said not to worry, it's just false labour pains."

Another pain came. It was even more intense. Then she felt a sudden *whoosh* and looked down to see that her water had broken. "Um...John, it's time!"

"Now?!"

"Yes! Now!" She yelled. A crowd was gathering around them to see what the commotion was all about.

"Someone, please call 911!" called John.

"I'm a nurse." A voice came from the group. "Let me help! Everyone move! Give me some space!" And with Jackie's consent, she began barking orders. "Grab some towels, some warm water and some scissors!" she yelled to the staff behind the counter. Then, to Jackie, "What's your name, Darlin'?"

"J-Jackie," Jackie replied as she gave herself over to the nurse's judgement.

"Okay, Dad." The nurse pointed to John, as she placed towels under Jackie's head. "I need you to hold Mom's hand and let her squeeze as hard as she needs to." She turned back to Jackie. "Now, I'm going to see how much you are dilated, okay Jackie?" But the baby's head was already crowning and the nurse grinned and said, "Okay, Mom and Dad, it's show time!"

"No, not here," Jackie protested, "I'm supposed to be in the hospital! I have a birth plan!"

"Well, I'm sorry, Sweetheart, but your baby has other ideas!! Now give me a big push!" And, with one more push,

and to the amazement of Dad,
the coffee shop was filled with the
cry of a newborn baby.

"It's a girl!" declared the
nurse.

Everyone was celebrating
the miracle they had just
witnessed. After cutting the cord,
John stood amazed at what God
had created. *I'm a father! She's
perfect!*

Fighting back tears, he
gave a kiss to Jackie and
whispered, "You're amazing! I
love you!" He wrapped the nurse
in a big, grateful hug. "I'll never

be able to thank you enough!
What's your name?"

"Abigail," she said, and the
paramedics escorted the new
family off to the hospital.

Jackie and John named
their new little daughter, Abigail
Lynne. She weighed 8lbs. 7oz.
and had tufts of dark hair and
bright blue eyes.

"She's the most beautiful
girl I've ever seen," he marvelled,
and smiled, looking up into
Jackie's eyes, "Well, apart from
her mother, of course!"

17

Tom and Sarah came to the hospital as soon as they heard the news. Jackie was happy to see Sarah. She was not happy to see Tom, but was polite for Sarah's sake.

"She's beautiful," said Sarah as she hugged John and Jackie. "Can I hold her?"

"Of course you can!"

Sarah turned to Tom to show him the baby and all he said was, "Don't get any ideas,

Sarah. I don't need you getting fat. No offence, Jennifer."

"It's Jackie!" Sarah snapped.

"Whatever," said Tom, "Anyway, Babe, we need to get going. I have stuff to do."

"Can't we stay just a few more minutes?" Sarah pleaded.

"You stay, I'm leaving." Tom stormed off.

Sarah stood with her head down for a second and then turned to look at Jackie and John.

They had a look of disbelief on their faces.

"Why do you put up with that?" John asked.

"He's just tired. He's not always like this," Sarah lied.

"I can drive you home if you want to stay and visit for a bit, Sarah."

"Thank you, but no, I should go. I'll check in on you guys tomorrow." And Sarah was gone.

As Sarah walked outside to see if Tom really had left her

stranded, tears of anger ran down her face. *Why was Tom so rude? All I wanted was to see my friends. It's never a problem if he wants to see his.* She was running out of excuses for him.

Sarah saw Tom sitting in the parking lot waiting for her. She debated whether she should get into the car or not. She was upset with Tom—sick of the way he treated her. But she couldn't help it, she had to give him a chance to explain himself.

"Finally!" Tom said as she got into the car.

"Why did you act like that, Tom? That was embarrassing and rude!" said Sarah. "I'm getting really sick of the way you treat me! I'm wondering if we should even be together. You don't act as though you want to be with me."

"Sarah!" Tom shouted. "I'm sorry, okay? I'm tired and I hate hospitals. You know I love you and want to be with you! I can't believe you would even question that. If you don't believe me, you're right—maybe we shouldn't be together."

"Oh, Tom. I'm sorry. I didn't mean to doubt you. I just wish you had been nicer to John and Jackie. It's a big day for them."

"Ya, and that was the other thing, Sarah. Why did you hug John? Do you want him or something?"

"Tom, my best friend just had his baby! Are you out of your mind?!" Sarah was exasperated. "Just take me home, Tom. I need some time to think!"

When Sarah got home, her mother met her at the door.

""I just went to meet you at the hospital. Jackie and John said that you and Tom had just left. Isn't Abigail beautiful?" Jen asked.

"Yes, she really is," said Sarah, still upset by what had happened with Tom.

"Sarah, what's going on?"

"Nothing," she said. She wanted to tell her mom what had happened, but what if they worked things out? She didn't want her mom to dislike Tom any more than she already did.

"It's Tom again, isn't it?"

"Mom, I don't want to talk about it right now." Sarah ran upstairs and cried into her pillow for a while. She had done everything she could to make him happy, but now he was creating a rift between her and the people that really loved her.

From time to time lately, she had been thinking about Tom's friend, Robbie. She and Robbie had been talking more frequently since the day they had met with Tom at the coffee shop. Robbie had told her about his plans to be a youth pastor. She

thought that was such a

refreshing thing to hear. He was

wholesome and very kind. She

could tell that he would never

treat a woman the way Tom did.

After she had let her mind wander

for a while thinking about Robbie,

she felt guilty and pushed those

thoughts to the back of her mind.

18

After they arrived home from the hospital, the reality of the situation really started to set in for Jackie. She knew that John—with all his heart—wanted this to work out; he wanted to provide for his little family. Sometimes he would even say not to worry about starting a career. "I'll provide for you and Abigail!" he would say. That just wasn't fair! He knew how badly Jackie wanted to be successful. She had a plan and she was having a really hard time seeing him and Abigail fitting into it.

John's mom was a big help with Abigail at first, when John was around, but when he left for school or work, she would change.

'You're going to get used to this, Jackie." Her mother-in-law kept saying. But Jackie would cry and say that it was all too much. Then, through tightened lips, her mother-in-law would snap, "Smarten up! Babies are a lot of work!" She often added: "You didn't mind *making* Abigail, now you need to *look after* her!"

Jackie would have called her own mom, but Barb was so busy working all the hours she could to support her boyfriend that she really didn't have a lot of time to talk.

Sarah was there for her but didn't have much to offer. She couldn't possibly understand what Jackie was going through. Sarah's parents would drop off diapers or formula sometimes, but they didn't feel it was their place to get too involved. On the outside, it looked like she had lots of support. And, when she tried to tell John about the way his mom was treating her, he just told her that she was being too sensitive.

"She loves you, Jackie. Anything she says is just to help!" John would say.

John's dad just did whatever he had to do to keep the peace in the house and that always meant that he went along with whatever John's mom decided was right.

Jackie felt completely trapped, trapped in a life that she

never wanted. These thoughts coursed through her, as they had since leaving the hospital. But, this time, she remembered something! Suddenly her body relaxed, her chin lifted. *Aunt Jane! ... Aunt Jane—my lifelong hero and mentor!* Jackie thought. *She has always invited me to come and stay with her in Vancouver anytime I might feel the need to get away. Maybe now's the time!*

19

John was in love with his new family. His parents and Jackie's mom had been wonderful. Even Sarah's parents had been really helpful. Everyone gave them tips on how to care for Abigail. But, no matter how helpful they all were, Jackie was no longer herself. She seemed to be angry all the time. She seemed to resent him and Abigail. John had thought that once Jackie had Abigail in her arms she would change.

But, if anything, she just got worse.

John did the best he could to keep up with school and he worked hard to support Jackie and Abigail. That meant that he wasn't around as much as he wanted to be, and that made everything more difficult. Jackie would hand Abigail off to any family member who would take her.

John thought that if he tried to be everything Jackie needed, he could make her happy. He was exhausting himself going to school, work, and then coming home to spend time with his little family. He tried to reassure Jackie about finishing school and starting a career.

"Don't worry, I'll support us!" He would say. No matter what he did it never seemed to be enough to make Jackie happy.

Jackie and Abigail had only been home from the hospital for a couple of weeks when John came home from work to find Abigail with his mom, and Jackie nowhere to be found. She had told Amanda that she had to go out for more diapers and simply never came home. In their bedroom, John found a note:

Dear John,

I'm so sorry! I just can't do this anymore. You will be fine without me. You're a great dad! I will always love you and I hope you can understand.

Love always,

Jackie

John ran upstairs in panic. "She's gone!"

"What do you mean, 'She's gone!'?" his mother yelled.

'Look! I found this note!"

"How can a mother leave her child?" she said under her breath as she read the note. "Call her mother, John. Maybe *she* will know where Jackie went."

John ran to the phone and called Jackie's mother. "Where is she?" he shouted.

"I'm so sorry, John. Jackie told me that she felt as if she was drowning…"

"What do you mean 'drowning'?" John fought back tears. He couldn't believe what was happening. He realized that she had become increasingly aloof but he didn't think she'd leave him and Abigail. "So where did she go?" he asked.

"She has an aunt in Vancouver and I paid for her ticket,"

"Can I have the phone number and address? When is she coming back?"

"I don't know, Honey, it was a one-way ticket. I'm so sorry, John. I couldn't stand to see her suffer. I wanted to tell you, but she begged me not to! I will be here to help with Abigail. Please let me keep seeing her," she pleaded.

"Phone number!" yelled John.

"She will contact you when she's ready," she said and slowly hung up.

174

John was devastated. "How could she leave us?" he cried to his parents. They just shook their heads.

"I did everything I could to help her," claimed his mother.

"How am I going to do this without her?!"

"You aren't alone, Honey. Your dad and I are here to help you."

That night, after John put Abigail to bed, he lay in his own bed and cried himself to sleep. He just didn't understand.

20

The day after Jackie left, Sarah got a frantic call from John.

"Did you know?" he asked.

"Did I know what?" Sarah was then devastated to hear that Jackie had left. "Why did she leave? Where did she go?"

"She went to stay with her aunt in Vancouver!" He tried not to cry but couldn't help it. Saying it out loud made it all too real.

"I'm shocked, John! I don't know what to say. I'm so sorry! I don't understand why she would leave!"

John took a deep, steadying breath. "She left a note saying that she couldn't handle this anymore. I don't even know what she was 'handling'—I've been doing everything I can to provide for her and make her happy. I know that she wasn't sure about keeping Abigail when she was pregnant, but I thought we were getting past all that. I thought we were happy! What am I going to do, Sarah?"

Sarah's heart was breaking for John and Abigail. She felt guilty that she had been so wrapped up in her own life with Tom that she hadn't noticed her friends' struggle. Life as she knew it was spinning out of control. She knew that Jackie wanted to focus on her future, but she couldn't have had anyone more supportive than John in her life.

"I'm here for you, John, however I can help. Your parents

will be a huge help and my parents are here, too. You aren't alone, John. Please remember that."

"Thanks, Sarah." John sighed and hung up.

Sarah tried to collect her thoughts after the startling news from John. She told her parents what had happened then called Tom, but–sobbing–she had to leave a message: "Tom, it's me! I really need to talk with you. Jackie left! I have no idea if I will even see her again!""

21

There had been talk around school the next morning that Jackie had left. When Robbie heard this, he immediately thought of Sarah. *I wonder how she's doing? She must be really upset! Poor John and baby Abigail!* He prayed for them the moment he heard the news.

Later that day, Robbie saw Tom in class. "Hey Tom, how is Sarah holding up?"

"With what?" asked Tom, without a clue.

"Didn't you hear about Jackie leaving?"

'Oh ya," he said, remembering the voicemail that Sarah had left him. 'I heard something about that."

"Well? Is Sarah okay? I'm sure she's upset about it!" Robbie was exasperated with Tom.

'Why would Sarah be upset?"

"Jackie's her best friend!" Robbie yelled.

"Okay, Dude, chill. I'll ask her tonight, okay? That's if she'll talk to me. We had a bit of a thing a couple days ago…"

Robbie rolled his eyes. What had Tom done this time?

"…she was mad when I wanted to leave the hospital the other night. I hate hospitals!" Then a light went on in Tom's head. He realized that he had gone too far at the hospital and that he needed to do something to win Sarah back. This fake concern about Jennifer…Jennifer?…no,

182

um...Jackie...would be just what he needed. "Thanks for telling me, Robbie."

Robbie suddenly realized that he had just given Tom the ammunition to win Sarah back: pretending to care. He should have just asked Sarah himself.

That evening, as Sarah and her parents were talking, there was a knock at the door. "I'll get it," said Sarah. It was Tom holding flowers.

"Hey, Sarah," he said, handing her the flowers. "Robbie

told me that he heard that Jackie had left. Are you okay?"

"Didn't you get my voicemail?"

"No," Tom lied.

Sarah's heart softened. *How sweet that Tom came over when he heard!* She was happy that Robbie had filled him in. She pushed her growing feelings for Robbie aside and gave Tom a huge hug. "Thank you for caring, Tom! And, thanks for the flowers. They're beautiful."

"No prob, Babe, I miss you. It hasn't been the same, not talking to you these last couple days," he replied.

"I miss you, too, Tom." She had already forgotten why she had been mad at him.

"Pick me up for school in the morning?" he reminded her, kissed her, and left.

When Sarah went back inside, she showed her parents her flowers. "Look at these flowers -aren't they beautiful? Tom gave them to me. It just goes to show that you really don't know people as well as you think you do!"

Her mom looked at her and slowly shook her head. She had been hoping that Sarah was starting to see through Tom, but he had some crazy hold over her. He kept drawing her back in!

22

When Jackie arrived in Vancouver, her aunt was there to greet her.

"Hi, Aunt Jane," called Jackie.

"Hi, Honey. How was your flight?"

"Good." Jackie tried to rein in all the thoughts that had been swirling in her mind throughout the trip. It was all just too much. She had done what she had to do!

"Are you hungry?" Aunt Jane asked.

"Um... a little."

They stopped to eat and made painful small talk. Jane wanted to ask what had happened, but she didn't want to push Jackie too soon. Jackie wanted to tell Jane everything and cry in her arms, but didn't know if she should—if she started crying, she might never stop. People were going to be talking about her at home, if they weren't already. She could imagine them saying things like, *How could she*

leave her baby? or *She had it all!*
How could she be so selfish?
Then, of course, there was
John...and Abigail. Jackie now
believed that she didn't know how
to be a good wife and a good
mom. She loved them both but
she just couldn't handle all the
responsibility. It was all too
distracting. She needed to focus
on her schooling. She had a plan
that they just didn't fit into.

Jackie's aching body
reminded her of what she had left
behind. She tried to focus on
other things. "What are high

schools like around here?" she asked Jane.

"Good. There's a really good one in my area. Does that mean you will be staying awhile?"

"Yes, I think so. If that's okay..."

"Of course it is. I'm happy to have you."

Aunt Jane had grown up in Niagara just like Jackie did. She always did well in school and after high school she became a very successful business woman. Her work took her all over the world. Jackie had always envied her Aunt Jane—the life she lived was so exciting. She never married—always said she didn't have time to settle down for any man. She would date but, as far as Jackie knew, it was never serious. Her first love was her work. She moved to Vancouver a couple of years ago and fell in love with the mountains and the ocean. She soon realized that she never wanted to live anywhere else. Her sister—Jackie's mom—would coax her to come home to Niagara but

Vancouver was now home, and that was that.

After dinner they returned to the house. Jackie was in awe as they came closer to the mountains.

"It's so beautiful here!" she said to Jane.

"Now you know why I never want to leave!" Jane smiled at the on-coming road and scenery.

When they pulled into Aunt Jane's driveway, Jackie was impressed with how modern it looked. The roof was built at odd peaks and angles. It was bright white with full walls of windows looking out onto the mountains. Inside Jackie peered through large glass sliding doors that led to a multi-level patio which overlooked a beautiful swimming pool and hot tub—all framed by those amazing mountain views. *I could get used to this,* she thought.

Jackie and Aunt Jane changed into comfy clothes and snuggled into the soft grey couch with cups of tea and a perfect view of the nature surrounding them.

Jane chose her timing carefully. "So, are you ready to fill me in, Jackie?

"Well—I had been going out with John for a while and things were going well," Jackie replied. "He was really good at giving me space when I needed to study. We had talked about our future and the possibility of getting married once our careers were underway. But then..."

"...But then, Abigail?"

"Yes, then I got pregnant. This just isn't what I want for my life right now. Maybe later, but not now. I told John that, too. I told him when I was pregnant that I thought we should put her up for adoption, but he wouldn't!" Jackie sobbed and grabbed a tissue. "So then I was stuck at home, exhausted, and even when I did go to school, I couldn't focus. Abigail needed me all the time. I know it's not her fault. I know… but I just can't handle it anymore. Then, there's John's mother. She pretends to be very supportive when John is around, but… when he's gone... she's mean... and yells at me all the time!"

"Wow! I'm sorry," replied Aunt Jane. "That does sound like a lot to deal with at your age. You felt that adoption was the best for all of you, but no one would listen. That's so awful!"

"Thank you for understanding, Aunt Jane!" Tears were streaming down Jackie's flushed cheeks. She felt drained from today's flight...and the past struggle.

"I think it's time to rest and we can talk more tomorrow."

Jane was wise enough to know when a conversation had run its course for the night.

The next morning, Jackie woke up to the fragrance of coffee wafting into her room. Last night had been her first full night of sleep in weeks. Her mind drifted to Abigail and John. She wondered how they were doing. Then she stopped herself. *I did what I had to do!* This was a new start. She was leaving the past behind.

Jackie found her aunt in the kitchen cooking eggs and bacon for their breakfast.

"I hope you're hungry, Jackie."

"Starving....

They sat at the table eating breakfast and making small talk, then Jackie headed to the beach for a walk in the crisp, spring air. The salty ocean breeze was caressing and refreshing. She looked upward and thought *this is just what I needed!*

Jackie had a lot on her mind. She was trying to figure out what life was going to look like for her now. She was sad that she had to go so far away from home, but home was tainted now. *I can never go back*, she thought! She was sad that she had left Sarah behind, too. Even though she knew that she had done what she needed to do, it wasn't easy. As she walked, she was finally able to feel all the emotions that made her run away. She felt angry with John for not hearing her. She had told him that she wasn't ready and he just kept saying that

199

everything would work out. She felt angry with his mother for being so awful to her. She also became aware of feelings of anger toward her own mom. *Why was Mom never there for me? It was always the men that came first—every time.* And, Jackie resented the fact that she, Jackie, would be portrayed as the bad guy. Abigail was a beautiful baby and Jackie loved her very much, but Jackie believed that she just couldn't be the mother Abigail needed.

Okay, that's enough, Jackie told herself. It was time to pick herself up and start making plans for her future. She walked back to the house and started preparing for registration at her new high school the next day.

Later that night, Jackie finally got up the courage to call Sarah. When she asked Aunt Jane if it would be okay, the reply was re-assuring:

"Of course, Honey! This is your home!"

23

Sarah was really worried about Jackie. When Sarah picked up Tom for school, she was not herself.

"What's wrong with you?" Tom asked.

"I'm worried about Jackie!" she responded, amazed that he even needed to ask.

"You're still on that?" Tom was annoyed. *Great,* he thought, *now I'm going to hear about this all day*."

"Yes, I'm still on that!" Sarah snapped, close to tears. "Jackie's my best friend and what she's going through must be difficult. Man! You're so insensitive, Tom!"

"I'm sorry. You're right, Babe," he replied. He knew he had pushed too far again.

"It's okay. I just wish she'd call me so I know she's okay."

When they arrived at school, Tom gave her a kiss and they went their separate ways to their lockers. On her way, she ran into Robbie.

"Hey, Sarah! How are you holding up?"

Sarah was touched that Robbie genuinely cared. He was so different from Tom. "Not great!" she replied, unable to hold back the tears. "I just don't understand what happened! Tom thinks that I should just let it go and not be upset, but I can't help it!"

"Of course, you can't. She's your best friend. I would imagine she's like family to you. I probably shouldn't say this ...I mean, Tom is my friend but he's kind of—uh—an idiot." As soon as he said it, he wanted to take back his words, unspoken. He just couldn't stand the thought of the woman he was falling in love with being treated that way.

Sarah felt a rush of emotions. She was touched, but at the same time she felt strangely defensive of Tom. "He's not that bad."

"Sorry, Sarah, I shouldn't have said that."

"No, it's okay, Robbie. I'll see you later." And she was gone. Sarah felt as if she was talking to the enemy. With the growing feelings she was having for Robbie, she felt guilty talking to him. Now Robbie was putting Tom down! Although she knew he was right, she wasn't the kind of person who could give up on someone. She had made a commitment to Tom. *He's not all bad*, she thought.

Later that night, Sarah finally heard from Jackie.

"Jackie?! Are you okay? What's going on?"

"Sarah, I'm sorry I left without telling you...I just had to go..."

"Where are you?"

"I'm at my aunt's in Vancouver. I'm staying here, Sarah. I can't go back to the Falls now. Too much has happened. I'm sorry..."

"Oh, Jackie! What happened? I'm so sorry that I wasn't there more for you!"

"No, it's not your fault, Sarah. It was John and his mom...and Abigail. John wouldn't listen to me when I told him–right

from the start–that I wasn't ready

for a baby. He wouldn't agree to

put her up for adoption–kept

telling me that it would all work

out! He kept saying that we would

have lots of help but there was

none. If he was home, his mom

would help; but when he wasn't,

she wouldn't. She would only yell

and scold me. I even had to beg

her to hold the baby when he

wasn't around. I had to beg her

to take Abigail just for an hour so

that I could run to the store the

day that I finally left. And my own

mother was never around. I

couldn't take it, Sarah! I don't want to be a teenage mom! It was not part of my plan!"

After Sarah hung up, she prayed for Jackie. She couldn't help being a little upset that Jackie had left, but she was really trying to understand. She wanted Jackie and John to be back together with Abigail. But, apparently, that wasn't going to happen.

Then Sarah's mind drifted to Tom and Robbie. She loved Tom, but Robbie was so much nicer to her. *But then, again, you don't really know someone until you're with them. Maybe Robbie has some deep, dark secrets*, she thought—but didn't really believe that. She felt guilty that she was falling for Robbie. *Just ignore it! We'll soon be out of high school and away from each other anyway.* But it was getting harder and harder to see Robbie in the halls. Their greetings to each other were getting warmer and more welcoming, and their conversations longer.

The longer Sarah thought, the more convinced she became

that she needed to make a decision about Tom—and about Robbie. She had a very strong suspicion that Robbie felt the same way she did. Maybe she needed to talk to Tom—without bringing Robbie into it. *I'll tell Tom our relationship is over...it's just not working anymore.*

24

John woke up to his living nightmare. Jackie really was gone! It hadn't been a dream. Abigail had been fussy all night.

"You miss you're mommy, don't you?" John whispered to her. He just couldn't figure out how he was going to play the role of both mom and dad. He'd have to figure it out. *Toughen up,* he told himself, *there is no other choice. Who knows when—if— Jackie will be back?!*

Later that morning, John called Sarah. Maybe she would know something. Sarah was just as shocked as he was. How could Jackie hide this from both of them? He could feel himself beginning to get angry. As he looked at Abigail, he couldn't imagine ever leaving her. How could her own mother just walk away like that?!

John's parents and Jackie's mom were a huge help. He was still able to attend school and go to work. He just cut his hours back a bit to spend more time with Abigail. But deep down he was really struggling. It had been a week now since Jackie left, and he was a mess. He tried to be strong, but it was very difficult.

Amanda, John's mom, kept asking him how he was really doing. All he would say was, 'I'm fine, Mom." He didn't want to add stress to her life. He knew it wasn't good for her multiple sclerosis. This was another reason he was angry with Jackie—she knew what this would do to his mom!

Abigail was changing every day—she was looking more and more like Jackie. *Ironic*, he thought. *I had hoped Abigail would look like Jackie, but now that she does, that's what hurts me the most.*

John longed to hear from Jackie to get an explanation of what happened...to yell, to cry! None of this was fair!

The days that followed at school were tough. People would whisper to each other when they saw John. "Isn't that the guy whose girlfriend left him with the baby?"   John would do his best not to react, but some days it seemed impossible to hold back. Sarah would stand up for him when she was there. Also, Robbie who was in a couple of his classes would frequently ask him how he was doing. Robbie even invited him to church a couple times and John was thinking about going. What did he have to lose?

25

Tom was in the middle of class when he was called to the office. His mom was there, crying.

"What's wrong?" Tom asked.

"It's your dad, Tom. He collapsed at work from a massive heart attack. I'm sorry, Honey. He's gone!"

Stunned, Tom continued. "What do you mean he's gone, Mom? Why couldn't anyone help him?!"

"They said it happened so fast that he was gone even before they could call 911."

Tom and his mom hugged each other and cried. It seemed so surreal to Tom that he kept asking if she was sure. Finally, when he regained his composure, he said, "I need Sarah."

The school secretary called Sarah out of class. When she arrived and saw Tom and his mother consoling each other, she rushed over to them. "What happened?"

"It's my dad! He's dead!"
And Tom and his mother
explained what had happened.

"I need to take care of
some of the arrangements for
him, Tom." Carole finally said.

Tom and Sarah insisted on
going with her. Sarah called her
mother to explain, adding "Please
pray for them!"

When they arrived at the
funeral home, Tom was too
distressed to focus and his mom
kept thanking Sarah for being
there. Sarah's heart was breaking
for them. It was such a huge loss

for Tom's family. Even though Jim wasn't always the nicest person, he was still Carole's husband and Tom's father. Tom's sudden dependence on Sarah surprised her. Maybe Tom had finally turned a corner. Maybe *they* had finally turned a corner together. *Maybe he finally sees that he needs to treat me better*, she thought.

The funeral went as well as could be expected. It was a very long day and Tom and his mother and Sarah were exhausted. Sarah's parents came to pay their respects and so did Robbie and his family. Even though she knew Robbie would be there at some point, her heart still skipped a beat when he walked in. *Forget about that*, she thought, *you're with Tom and he needs you.* He came and spoke with Carole, Tom, and Sarah, and gave Carole a hug before leaving. *How sweet and caring*, Sarah thought.

The days that followed were very hard for Tom and his mom. Carole had not worked in the seventeen years she and Jim had been married. Jim had life insurance but that wouldn't last long with bills to pay. Tom would need a job to help out.

"Do you think your dad would hire me, Sarah?" Tom asked.

Her dad was not a big fan of Tom, but maybe this would be a way for them to get to know each other better. "I'll ask him tonight."

That night when Sarah got home, she talked to her dad. "Do you think we could hire Tom at the shop? They could really use the money."

"H-m-m-m-m. Well, what do you think he could do?"

"He could do manual labour...whatever you need him to do. It would give you a chance to get to know him better, too."

Greg found it hard to say *no*, considering the circumstances. But he was still not keen on the idea. "Yep, we can give him a chance. But, if it doesn't work out, he's gone. Okay?"

"I'm sure it will, Dad. Thank you." Sarah ran upstairs to call Tom. "Dad says he'll hire you!"

"Oh....that's great....thanks, Babe. I won't have to work weekends, will I? I still want some time for myself."

Sarah felt the disappointment she had felt so many times before with Tom. "I'm not sure, Tom. I thought you'd just be happy to have a job!"

"Why are you being like that? I'm happy. I just don't want to be tied down all the time."

Sarah realized that getting Tom to work for her dad was going to be a mistake. Greg Sanders would not put up with that kind of attitude. "Hey! At least if you *do* work weekends, we can work together!"

"Ya, I see you enough. I need my own time to do what I want sometimes," he replied.

"Right," Sarah snapped. *What am I going to do*? she thought. She was so sick of the way he treated her. She did everything she could to make him happy, but nothing was ever good enough. What did he mean: he needed his time? She never got her own time! Now she was stuck—how could she leave a guy who just lost his dad? Plus, now he might be working for her dad! What a mess! All the while, she kept thinking of Robbie and how different she knew life could be with him. She needed to talk to her best friend. She needed Jackie.

26

When Robbie got the news about Tom's dad, he was stunned. It hadn't been that long ago that he had spoken with Jim at the store! Robbie felt terrible for Tom and his mom. He liked Carole and had always felt that she got the raw end of the deal in her marriage. Now, Robbie prayed for them that they would be okay. He reassured Tom that he'd be there for whatever they needed.

Robbie felt guilty that his feelings for Sarah were growing over time. He also felt that those feelings were becoming mutual—that is, until Tom's dad died. Now he felt even worse, having those feelings when Tom had just lost his dad! At the same time, he knew how badly Tom treated Sarah. If only she knew the truth about Tom! Robbie knew that Tom had been unfaithful to Sarah from time to time. But Robbie didn't think it was his place to tell her. He kept telling Tom to come clean, but Tom had it way too good to ruin it now.

Now that Robbie was in his last year of high school, he was focusing even more on which Bible college he wanted to attend. Maybe going somewhere further away would be a good idea. He couldn't stand the thought of running into Tom and Sarah anymore. If things worked out in a few months, he could be gone and not have to worry anymore. He sent out applications to a few schools and was thrilled to be accepted by his top two choices. One was only an hour away, but the other was miles away in

Saskatchewan. He was really leaning towards Saskatchewan.

Robbie's thoughts also turned toward his graduation prom. He knew his mother looked forward to having prom pictures of her boys with their dates. He couldn't let her down...but who would he bring? *Great,* he thought, *something else to worry about!*

Over the years, Robbie had made some great friends at Youth Group. One night, halfway through his grade 12 year, Rebecca Johnson showed up at

Youth Group. She was a beautiful girl with long brown curly hair cascading over her shoulders. She was average height and build, with blue eyes and a smile that could light up the room. Robbie always wanted people to feel comfortable, so he took her under his wing and they had become good friends. He really liked having her as a friend. It was nice to feel that he could be himself and not self-conscious as he was with other girls. Since there were no thoughts of dating each other, the pressure was off.

"Robbie, is Rebecca your girlfriend?" Mrs. James once asked. She really liked Rebecca— always polite when she came to visit.

"No, Mom, we're just friends," Robbie had said, annoyed that if he hung out with a girl they had to be 'together' in other people's eyes.

One day as the prom loomed closer, Robbie decided to ask Rebecca to go with him.

"Like a date?" asked Rebecca nervously.

"No, not as a date, as friends." They both breathed a sigh of relief and laughed.

"Okay, on one condition," Rebecca said, smiling: "You come to mine, too."

"Oh, sure!"

In the Johnson home, it was also prom time for Rebecca's sister, so the two girls were sharing the excitement of shopping and getting ready together. Rebecca looked enchanting in a floor-length black lace dress with a brown underlay and brown heels. Her sister's

233

shorter, dark blue dress dazzled with her long blonde hair. Rebecca's mom looked at them with tears in her eyes. "I can't believe my girls are growing up so fast," she said, while 'her girls' laughed and rolled their eyes–as they always did when their mom got all mushy.

Robbie had rented his suit with his mother's and Rebecca's help–"to make sure they would be picture perfect." He picked up Rebecca amidst a flurry of excitement and picture-taking, and they headed off to an evening of fun. By the end of the night, their mothers would have the prom pictures they were looking forward to, and Robbie and Rebecca could focus on the future.

27

Rebecca Johnson had grown up in foster care until she was 5 years old. She didn't know a lot about her birth parents except that they were very young when she was born. Her first foster home was in St. Catharines, with a couple who were told that they would never conceive. But just as they started the adoption process for Rebecca, the wife found out that she was pregnant. The couple decided that it would be too overwhelming to have both

Rebecca and their own baby,

so—just a few months old—

Rebecca was returned to foster

care. Due to a series of

unfortunate events, she was

placed with family after family

until, finally, she found a loving

Christian forever-home, at the

age of five.

Her new parents already

had three children. They said

they then felt God telling them to

adopt. When they got word that

Rebecca needed a home, they

knew she was going to be their

child. They spent a lot of time praying that their biological children would be very accepting of any other child they brought into their family. The children were included in the planning so they never felt left out. Rebecca and her sister, Lynne, were the same age and that worked out well for both of them. There were times when they fought like normal siblings do, but for the most part they were best friends. The two boys, Jacob and Johnathan, were 7 and 11years old, when Rebecca arrived. They vowed to protect their sisters and to always be there for them. Although they sometimes waivered–as siblings often do– they formed a very close family. The fact that Rebecca was adopted was never kept from her. Her parents would tell her that she had been chosen to be their daughter. With them, she felt that she was loved and treated equally with her siblings.

Although life was good for Rebecca, it was not without its challenges. It always seemed that she had a harder time learning to read than the other kids.

"Why do you find it hard to read?" her mom would ask her.

"I don't know. All the letters are just mixed up," Rebecca would respond. Her parents took her to several eye doctors and they all said that her eyes were fine. Finally, in grade 3, her teacher suggested that she be tested for dyslexia. Sure enough, she was right! Having the diagnosis didn't make reading any easier, but it did provide her with the teaching support to help her understand what she was reading. Because of this,

Rebecca couldn't help feeling that she was a nuisance. She was always afraid that her parents would put her back into foster care. Even though her new family would try to reassure her, in the back of her mind Rebecca continually felt the need to try extra hard to keep everyone happy.

The need to please would prove to be troublesome as Rebecca got older. Boys would take advantage of her kind and giving nature. At the end of a relationship, she would always

241

feel used and thrown aside. It hurt, but she would try to have hope and faith that there was a good person out there for her. Thankfully, she had made good friends over the years and they were very supportive. During grade 12, her family switched churches to find one that had more to offer their children. Rebecca and her siblings fit in immediately and enjoyed their weekly youth group.

It was at Youth Group that Rebecca met Robbie. He made her feel comfortable the moment she walked through the door for the first time. As she got to know him better, she could tell he was going to be a really good friend. He was the first guy she had met in a long time, who didn't have any other agenda except to be friends. It was refreshing.

28

Tom felt as though he was walking in a fog. Since his dad died everything was different. People looked at him differently at school. They had sympathy in their eyes when they talked to him. His home was strangely silent when he came home from school every day. He felt alone. His dad had been the only one who really understood him. Now, no one did.

Carole, his mother, was starting to find her own voice for the first time. She was starting to take steps—though wobbly at first—toward making a new life without her husband. After 17 years, it felt scary, but she did have some administrative experience from her previous career to build on. She started asking everyone she knew about possible job openings and would submit resumes—it seemed, everywhere. Finally, she got a job with a local law firm for a little more than minimum wage.

Carole was also trying to step into the role of the authority figure of the house, but she was quickly seeing that—when it came to Tom—the damage had already been done, a long time ago. He didn't respect her. As much as she didn't want to have to be the bad guy, she simply could not afford to support herself and him on the limited budget she had.

"You need to get a job, Tom!" she would say.

"There's nothing I want to do!" he would yell at her.

"Well, either find something and start contributing or you'll have to find somewhere else to live!" Carole would say, shaking with anger.

Sarah had told Tom that her dad had said he would hire him. Tom hoped he would like it there—he didn't want to have to do any kind of work that got him dirty. *Is Sarah even trying?* he thought. *Why is she not offering to pay for something over here?* Of course, in Tom's mind, it was everyone else's fault.

"Have you found any job possibilities?" asked Tom's mom one day. Her stress was obvious.

'Not yet. I asked Sarah if her dad would hire me, but I don't even know if I want to do that kind of work. It's not fair that I should have to, anyway!" he yelled.

"Well, none of this is fair!" his mother yelled back. "Do you think I wanted your father to die and leave us with nothing?"

With that, Tom stomped to his room and slammed the door. Carole burst into tears. This had become a constant exchange between them since the funeral, and the tension continued to grow.

Tom had been avoiding Sarah's calls all morning. It was Saturday and he really didn't feel like talking. Plus, she would probably be expecting him to go over to her place and see what job her dad might have for him. He wasn't up to that today. His mom had left for some training at her workplace that day so he had the house to himself. *I think I'll call that chick I met last weekend,* he thought and proceeded to set up a date with her for just a few minutes later.

He spent the afternoon with his date until him mother came home.

"Hi Tom, hi Sarah!" his mom called as she came into the house and heard voices in the living room.

"Who's Sarah?" asked the girl on the couch, jumping up to make a quick exit.

"She's nobody!" hollered Tom.

Tom's mom just stood in shock watching what was transpiring. She knew that Tom was not good for Sarah, but she didn't think he'd stoop this low!

"Who was that?!" his mom demanded to know after the girl stormed out.

"She's just a friend! Thanks for making her feel uncomfortable!"

"H-m-m-m... You two were sitting much too close to be just friends!"

"Whatever, Mom! You don't know what you're talking about!" Then Tom stormed out, too.

"Where are you going?" she called after him.

"Out!" was all she could hear.

After Tom left, Carole just sat on the couch and cried. She knew his father had not been the best example, but she had hoped at least *something* good in her would have rubbed off on him over the years. She really didn't know what to do about him. /

guess I really will have to kick him out, she thought. *But then where will he go? Will he just get into trouble? Or might he mature a bit and clean up his act?* She also didn't want him to become poor Sarah's problem. That girl had a good head on her shoulders until it came to Tom. Things were so stressful already! He was eighteen and would be finishing high school in a couple months. Carole had no idea what to do.

Tom left the house feeling angry! *How dare she question what I was doing?* he thought.

What does it matter to her? It's not her life, it's mine! Things at home had been tense since his dad had died. They had been tense before that, too, but it was easier to ignore when he could just let his dad do the arguing and Tom could just retreat to his room. He really did love Sarah—just needed a break sometimes. His mom would never understand that. Those other girls meant nothing to him. Since his afternoon was ruined, he thought he might as well go and see Sarah.

29

Jen and Greg had a long talk about their carpentry business. They were thinking about putting it into Sarah's name. They knew Sarah was smart and could really add a lot to the business. The only issue they had was Tom.

'There's no way we can let her support him!" said Jen.

"Yes, I totally agree." Greg scowled and nodded his head.

"Well, how do we handle this without losing her? She has been so defensive when it comes to Tom that anytime I even bring up his name, she bites my head off!"

"I'm not sure we can tell her that she has to choose between either Tom or the business at this point—she would probably choose *him*." Greg ran his hand across his forehead in frustration.

"Why don't we tell her that one of the legal obligations of any of the partners is to have a prenuptial agreement drawn up?" Jen thought out loud. "Regardless of who she marries, it's just what's required. It's out of our hands that way."

"Perfect!"

30

With Jackie gone, John was feeling a lot of emotions. Sometimes he was angry—angry at Jackie for leaving...at himself for not seeing the signs...at the whole situation. Did Jackie really think this is what he signed up for? He had not imagined his life turning out this way! He had never pictured himself as a father at the age of sixteen, but he was mature enough to realize that life is often the sum of the choices made. He had made his bed and now he had to lie in it! It was never an option for him to run away like Jackie did, leaving them to fend for themselves. When Jackie first left, he would have done anything to get her to come home. Now, after a couple months, he was so angry that he didn't think he would want her home at all!

There were nights that he lay awake with Abigail beside him and he could hear his parents talking about Jackie.

"I still can't believe that she really left," his mom would say.

"Well, yes, I know...it's hard to know what was going on in her head, being so young. She always talked about her big plans. She had everything figured out...all the time. Let's face it: John was just around for the ride. It wasn't a real relationship—it was John being controlled by Jackie," his dad would say.

John would hear this and it hurt to think that might be true. Looking back on their relationship he had always just let Jackie have her way. He did his best to make her happy. Why couldn't she just be happy? He thought he had done everything right but he wasn't arrogant enough to think he was always right. He just didn't understand. He wished Jackie would talk with him—even just once—to explain her side. But then again, right now he might be too angry to even listen. He just felt lost. He felt abandoned with no time to figure things out because he had a baby to care for. Their baby! How could she have left their beautiful little girl?

John cried for Abigail. He would do anything for her to not

have to grow up without her mother. How was he going to explain her mother's leaving to her when she got older? To think that her mother didn't want her! Jackie had put them both in a difficult and hurtful situation.

Then there were the looks he was still getting at school. His classmates didn't know how to talk to him anymore. Or maybe *he* didn't know how to talk to *them*. He had forgotten what it was like to be a typical teenager. He had forgotten what it was like to be carefree and only worry about himself. Most people his age didn't have to worry about making sure their baby hadn't drooled on their shirt before they hurried off to school. Other teenagers didn't have to ask their parents to babysit so they could go for a coffee. His world had changed from deciding on which colleges he would enjoy attending next year, to investigating which colleges offered child care!

`

Oh, and then there was the whole issue of graduation. John's classmates were talking about what they would wear to the prom and the after-parties. He was left wondering if he would even go. *Is it possible that I've outgrown it all, already?* Not only did he have Abigail to worry about, but he also had the memories of Jackie and him discussing attending those events together. His parents had encouraged him to go anyway and had offered to babysit Abigail. He would have to think about it.

One Saturday afternoon, John remembered that Robbie had given him his phone number and told John to call if he ever just wanted to get out of the house and go for coffee and talk. Even if he needed to bring Abigail, Robbie had said, that would be cool. In John's opinion, that was amazing. Aside from Sarah, Robbie was the only other person his age who had reached out and included Abigail. Well, the only one who had reached out at all!

John found Robbie's number and called. "Hey, Robbie, it's John. You had mentioned

going for coffee sometime. Are
you free today?"

"Ya, sure! We can go now
if you want. Do you mind if my
friend, Rebecca, tags along? She
and I were planning to meet at
the coffee shop in just a few
minutes, too."

"No, not at all. Do you
mind if I bring Abigail?" asked
John.

"Nope, all good! Rebecca
will love that!"

"Okay, I'll meet you there in ten...oh, make it twenty minutes."

It felt so strange taking Abigail to the coffee shop where she was born. John hadn't been back there since. He stopped to replay that day—as he had done a million times. Then he gave his head a shake and started to get ready. "Okay, we need diapers...wipes.....bottle..." he quickly packed the shoulder bag. "We're ready, Abigail!" And they were off to see Robbie and Rebecca.

When they got to the coffee shop, John and Abigail were greeted with delight by the staff who had been working there on the night she was born.

"Oh, look! She's so cute!" they oo-ed and aw-ed.

"So nice of you to take her out and give mom a break!" one well-intended lady said.

"Well, as a matter of fact, her mom left us," John replied.

"Oh, my goodness! I'm so sorry!" the lady said. "Well, I can tell that you are a great dad and that you two are going to be just fine!" and she turned to leave.

"Thank you, Ma'am."

By then, Robbie and Rebecca had come to his side.

"Well, that was awkward!" said John when they were all seated at the table. "Sorry about that!"

"Nothing to be sorry about," replied Robbie, as Rebecca nodded in agreement.

"She is such a beautiful little girl!" Rebecca remarked.

John would have loved to say, "Yes, she looks just like her mother." Given the circumstances, he didn't want to give Jackie that much credit.

John, Robbie and Rebecca had a great time talking and laughing. Since Jackie had left, this was the first John had been anywhere without feeling judged by those around him. He had not spoken with Robbie all that much at school, aside from Robbie asking him a couple of times how he was doing. John remembered Sarah and Jackie mentioning that Robbie was a friend of Tom's. The way Sarah talked about Tom, he wondered why she didn't dump the jerk and date Robbie. *But then, what do I know about girls anyway?!*

"So, how do you guys know each other?" asked John.

"We go to the same church," replied Robbie.

"Oh, very cool. I've never been to church."

"You're welcome to come to ours!" said Rebecca and Robbie at the same time. "Jinx!"

they chuckled to each other. It was then that John noticed what a pretty smile Rebecca had.

Abigail had fallen asleep in the car on the ride over and had slept while Rebecca, Robbie and John talked. Suddenly she started to wake up.

"May I hold her?" Rebecca asked. "I love babies!"

"Sure!" John took her out of her car seat and handed her to Rebecca. He noticed what a natural Rebecca was as she rocked Abigail back and forth and calmed her fussing.

"Would you like me to give her her bottle?" Rebecca offered.

John handed the bottle to Rebecca and, with that, Abigail settled into Rebecca's arms. John was amazed. Even his own mother had not had that effect on Abigail. He couldn't help but notice how beautiful and natural Rebecca looked holding the baby. *Incredible!*

31

Sarah's parents eventually sat Sarah down and discussed with her how they were going to restructure their business. They were going to make her a partner! She was over the moon at the thought of it. She tried to reach Tom all that day to tell him the news, but he hadn't answered his phone.

"I wonder what he's up to," she thought. She had had her suspicions lately, but she usually pushed them aside, telling herself that she was becoming paranoid. *But there was that one day last week though...* she thought. It had seemed strange that Tom hadn't answered on a day that she knew he was home. When he did finally answer, she heard a strange girl's voice in the background. She had asked who that was, and he had said that it was one of his mother's friends. She had found that odd but tried to let it go.

Tom finally showed up at Sarah's house later that afternoon.

"Tom, where have you been?!" Sarah had asked.

"Just hanging out at home. I didn't feel like talking."

"Oh. Well, guess what! I have some news!" She told him about the business partnership and his face lit up. *Wow!* she thought. *He's finally taking an interest in something that I'm interested in!*

"When will this take effect? Will you be getting a steady paycheck from this?"

"I'm not sure of all the details yet, but it's definitely exciting!"

"Yes, it is. Hey, have you had dinner yet? Maybe we could go out?"

"That would be great!" Sarah beamed with happiness.

Tom said they needed to celebrate so they went to one of the fancier restaurants. He ordered the steak. Sarah thought, *why not–we're celebrating!* Sarah ordered the less-expensive chicken and throughout the meal wondered how Tom was going to pay for this. Then it occurred to her that he hadn't volunteered to pay, he had just volunteered to eat! She didn't say anything because she was hoping he would surprise her...then the bill came. The only surprise was that he didn't even pretend that he was going to pay. Sarah panicked. She didn't know if she had enough money to pay for all of this.

"Tom, I thought since it was your idea, that you were going to pay! I don't have enough to cover all of this!" Sarah cried.

"It's okay, Babe." Tom pulled a wad of bills from his wallet.

"You mean you actually had the money to pay...and you were going to make me pay for everything again?"

"Well you're the one with the business!"

Sarah was seething. That was it. She'd had it with him. "Take me home, Tom!"

"What's your problem? It's true, isn't it?" He said smugly.

"You know how hard things have been for mom and me."

"Ya, I guess." Sarah hated fighting and she hated the fact that he would always turn arguments around to make her feel bad.

"Are you going to be mad at me all night?" he asked Sarah.

In a weak whisper, she said, "...no."

32

Jackie was getting comfortable living in Vancouver. All that she had left behind was becoming a slightly distant memory. Her room at Aunt Jane's was like her own getaway. She had a big window-with-a-view in her bedroom and an ensuite bathroom with a huge soaker tub.

Jackie was now registered at her new high school to start classes the following Monday. She had seen a few of her new classmates around her neighborhood. They all seemed very interested in the new girl. Jackie had been so focused on running away and making a fresh start that she had not thought about how difficult it might be. She was never one to have secrets, but now her whole life seemed like one. She couldn't tell people what had really happened. They would never understand. She had run away from things many people dream of having—a loving, devoted husband and a beautiful, healthy baby. She would need to be careful not to let anyone get too close.

Jackie had met a nice guy named Brad who lived next door to her aunt. They had said *hi* to each other a couple times. Although she did find Brad to be really attractive with his tall and muscular build, blonde hair and bright blue eyes, she was not going to pay any attention. She had to keep her guard up. She had promised herself that this was a new start. Never again was she going to let someone distract her.

Brad had noticed her, too. Aunt Jane laughed every time they drove home and Brad would wave to her. Jackie really hoped they wouldn't have any classes together.

Jackie had chosen lots of heavy courses to help her get ready for her career. The principal was allowing her to pick up where she had left off at home before she had Abigail. That meant she had some catching up to do, but she would get it done. She needed to stay focused.

"What do you think of me?" Jackie asked her Aunt Jane one morning.

Without hesitation, Aunt Jane replied, "I love you. You are bright, beautiful, goal-driven—"

"Even after everything I've done?!"

"Yes, Jackie, it was a very hard situation you were in...and such a young mother...and not being heard..."

"That's reassuring, Aunt Jane. Thanks for understanding." Jackie hoped that if her secret should ever come out in her new community, people would understand.

Jackie's first day at her new school was a crazy one. First of all, there was a downpour early in the morning. She had planned to walk to school, but now Aunt Jane had to drive her which meant that Jane had to rearrange her own schedule. Then, when Jackie finally arrived and started looking for her locker, she got lost. Who came to her aid? The one and only Brad, of course.

"Hey! Are you lost?" Brad asked, coming up behind her.

Great! Just what I need, she thought as soon as she heard his voice. "Yes, I'm lost. But I have a map, I'll figure it out." She hoped he'd just go away.

"Well, what's your locker number?" he asked.

"1011."

"Okay, that's upstairs by mine! Follow me! And he was off.

Great! Just great! Jackie tried to keep up with Brad as he ran up the stairs.

"Well, look at that. We're four lockers away from each other." Brad seemed thrilled.

"Yes, look at that." Jackie was a little less thrilled.

"I have to get to class. Are you good from here?"

"Yes, I think I'm good. Thanks for your help, Brad."

As Jackie made her way to grade 12 English, she hoped she wasn't too far behind everyone. She had missed three weeks of school by this point. When she walked into the classroom, she was introduced quickly by the teacher to the class, and then settled down to work.

"Hey, Jackie," whispered a girl in the desk beside Jackie.

"Hey!" returned Jackie cautiously.

"Welcome. I'm Jennifer."

"Thanks. Nice to meet you, Jennifer." When Jackie had arrived at the school that morning, she had thought the hardest thing was going to be focusing on her work and getting caught up. But she now realized

that dealing with the guilt and
shame that had followed her here
would probably be even harder.
Seeing new people eagerly
wanting to get to know her just
made her feel worse. She
wondered if they would be turning
their backs on her if they knew
the truth about what she had
done.

When it was lunch time,
Jackie made her way to the
cafeteria. She was thankful that
Aunt Jane had given her some
money that morning. While she
was standing at the lunch

counter, Jennifer came up beside her. "Hey, Jackie. Come sit with us."

"Us?"

"Ya. My cousin and a few friends and me." Jennifer explained.

"Okay. Cool. Thanks!" Jackie was relieved that she wouldn't have to sit alone. She pushed all the other feelings aside for now. Right now she was just 'Jackie, the new girl', that no one knew anything about. She would keep it that way for as long as she could.

"This is my cousin, Brad," said Jennifer when they reached the table. Jennifer had no idea that they already knew each other.

"We've met already," Jackie and Brad both laughed. And everyone around the table introduced themselves.

"So, where are you from?" asked Brad.

"Niagara Falls."

"Oh, I've heard it's really nice there!" "What's it like living so close to the falls?" others asked.

"Not as exciting as the mountains here! When you see the falls all the time, they lose their wonder a bit."

And the others agreed that the same can happen living near their beautiful mountains.

That afternoon, after school, the weather had cleared so Jackie was looking forward to a chance to walk alone and clear her head, but Brad appeared.

"Hey, Jackie! Mind if I walk with you?" he asked.

"Um, no, I guess not." She tried not to sound annoyed.

"So, how was the first day?"

"Pretty good, I think. Everyone seems so friendly."

"They are. Sometimes we go over to the coffee shop after school, if you're ever interested."

Wow, that sounds familiar, thought Jackie. "Um...maybe, sometime."

When Jackie got home her aunt was still at work—a perfect time to call Sarah. Sarah was glad to hear from her, but her heart sank as she listened to Jackie talk about Vancouver and her first day of school. *Jackie isn't coming back!* Tears welled up in Sarah's eyes. "I miss you, Jackie," she blurted out.

"I miss you, too! What's been going on with you?" So Sarah told her about her parents restructuring their business and putting her name on it as a partner. She talked about Tom and his father's death and how excited Tom was about her becoming a partner in the business. *I bet he is*, thought Jackie, *he's excited for himself!*

"Speaking of Tom," Sarah hurriedly added, "he's on his way to get me, so I'd better go. Talk to you soon, Jackie."

"Okay. Sounds good!" And the conversation was over.

Life goes on just fine without me, thought Jackie as she ended the call. All of a sudden she felt lonely. She tried to call her mom but, of course,

she wasn't home and Jackie
ended up having to make
conversation with her mom's
loser boyfriend. *Ugh*, she thought,
I won't do that again! Then she
remembered Brad's invitation for
coffee. She put her shoes back
on and walked over to his house.
Before she could knock, he
opened the door.

"What! Do you just sit
looking out the window?" Jackie
joked.

"Maybe." Brad was
laughing. "No, I was just about to
head out for a coffee...you wanna

join me?" And they hopped into his little red Toyota Corolla and headed over to the coffee shop. "Everyone I called was busy, so I was just going to get take-out and go for a drive. Is that cool?"

"Uh, sure..." Jackie's palms started to feel clammy. She felt nervous being alone with a guy she didn't really know. But, at the same time, it was nice having someone to talk with.

They drove for a while talking about what they wanted to do after high school. Brad wanted to be a mechanic. Jackie wanted to work for a big corporation–like her aunt did–and travel the world.

"Those are some big aspirations!" Brad briefly glanced from the road to her.

"Well, when you're focused, you can achieve anything!" Those were the words Jackie had told herself a million times before.

"Yes, for sure," agreed Brad. "So what brought you out here?"

Oh no! I knew this would come up—I just don't know how to answer!

Brad seemed like a great, easy going guy...but he was one of her few friends out here so far. If she told him the truth, he might turn away. But then, she didn't want to live a lie.

"Well, it's a long story, Brad, and I'm not proud of it..."

"We've got time..." replied Brad.

Jackie took a deep breath and paused for a few minutes to

think. *Once it's out there, it's out there,* she thought, *the words can't be taken back.* She hadn't anticipated connecting with people—especially a nice guy—so quickly.

"This is really hard to talk about," she said, "but I think I need to. I won't...uh... blame you...if you don't...want to talk to me after!"

33

Sarah was settling into life without her best friend. Jackie had been gone for a while now and their communication was limited. She had talked with John a lot lately and had noticed him hanging around Robbie at school. She was happy to see John making good friends and being such a great dad to Abigail.

Sarah was very excited about the future. Being a partner in the family business meant that the question that recently was never far from her mind—*what am I going to do after high school?*—had already been answered for her. Now she could just focus on taking business courses in college. Maybe some carpentry courses, too.

Tom was very excited for her, too. He was showing a real interest in her career. Sarah was surprised how much he seemed to care. He even showed up once to see about working with her dad. But, he was still undecided about what he wanted to do in life.

As Sarah grew more and more enamored of Tom, Jen and Greg became more and more disgusted by him. One Sunday afternoon while Sarah was up in her room listening to music, Jen and Greg were deep in discussion.

"What does she see in him?" Jen threw her arms up in exasperation.

"I really don't know." Greg sighed.

"Do you think we should have given her an ultimatum regarding the business?"

304

"I'm not sure, Jen. All I know is that I don't trust him one bit! I know that the only reason he is still around is that she told him that she'd soon be a partner in the business. The guy's a loser!"

Just then Sarah marched in. Her parents hadn't noticed that she had turned down the music in her room and was listening to them. "You're talking about Tom, aren't you?!" she shouted.

"Well...yes, Honey! We are!" Jen replied. "We don't trust him! We don't want him anywhere near you or our business!"

Sarah felt her world beginning to fall apart. "Why are you saying this?!" she cried. "How can you be so heartless! He just lost his dad. He's just trying to find his way. H-H-He loves me!"

"Sarah..." Jen blurted out, 'if he really loved you, he would be here supporting you! All he does is take from you and make you feel bad! I think it has to come down to this: it's either Tom or the business, Honey. You're going to have to choose."

'Dad, do you feel this way, too?" Sarah asked with the same

look she had had on her face when she found out that the Easter bunny wasn't real.

"I'm sorry, Sarah, but yes, I agree with your mother. We just don't trust him," replied Greg.

"Well, what about me? Don't you trust me?!" screamed Sarah.

"Of course, we do! But he can manipulate you. He's really good at that!" replied Jen.

"Well, if that's how little you really think of me, you can

keep your business!" Sarah stormed out.

"That went well!" said Greg sarcastically.

"I need to go after her!"

"No, Jen, give her time to cool off."

Sarah started walking and ended up at the coffee shop. She went to the payphone in front of the coffee shop to call Tom. She needed to talk to him right away, more than ever.

"Hello?" Carole's voice answered at the other end.

"Hi, Mrs. Brown. It's Sarah. May I speak with Tom, please?"

"No, I'm sorry, Honey, he's not here. I thought he was with you."

"Nope, I haven't seen him all–" as Sarah spoke, she spotted Tom in one of the booths inside, holding hands with a girl she didn't recognize...and he was kissing her Sarah was so surprised that she dropped the phone. Carole was still talking but Sarah didn't notice. Panic began to rise in her chest. *Do I go in and confront him? Do I just pretend that I didn't see anything? And*

how do I face Mom and Dad?

Maybe there's a reasonable

explanation...but they were

kissing! She fell to her knees on

the cold, wet pavement. She had

done everything for him! He really

was a loser! She didn't know

what to do. She didn't have

Jackie's new phone number with

her, but then remembered that

Robbie had given her his number

when Tom's dad died, in case he

could be of help. It might still be

in her jacket pocket. Her fingers

found that torn, lined paper.

Sarah pulled herself up off her

knees and grabbed the phone again. She dialed Robbie's number. She didn't know what she would say—she just knew she needed a friend right now.

34

"Hello," said a woman's voice.

"Hi, Mrs. James. Is Robbie there, please?" Sarah's heart was pounding. As she stood there at the payphone, she could still see everything that was going on inside the coffee shop.

"Hello?" Robbie was a bit out of breath.

"Hi Robbie, it's—"

"Sarah?"

"Yes, it's Sarah..." She was sobbing uncontrollably. 'I'm at the coffee shop... I just had a big fight with my parents... Tom's here with another girl and they've been kissing and holding hands... I'm outside at the payphone and I'm not sure what I should do!"

Robbie was filled with rage. The love he had for Sarah—that he had tried to ignore for so long—rose to the surface. "I'll come there! Just stay out of his sight and I will be right over!"

"Okay." Sarah was relieved, and thankful to have

someone on her side. She knew she would have to tell her parents that they had been right all along.

Robbie got to Sarah in record time.

"Sarah!" he called.

"Hey, Robbie! Thanks for coming!" Sarah was so relieved that she gave him a hug.

"Has Tom come out yet?"

"No. They're right there. See?" Sarah pointed to a booth inside.

There was Tom—plain as day—with a girl. Robbie was seething with anger. He was not a violent person but seeing Tom's cruel disregard for the women he claimed to love made Robbie sick.

"Do you want me to go in there, Sarah?"

"No." She had finally seen Tom for what he was. Everyone had warned her, including Robbie.

"Well, we can't just stand out here. What would you like to do? Do you want me to take you home? Or do you want to go grab something to eat somewhere?

"I'd love that, Robbie." Sarah's tears of betrayal and anger now turned into tears of gratitude. "You know something, Robbie? Tom and I have been together for—I don't know—five months, and he has never done anything for me like you did tonight!."

"*Any* friend would have done the same, Sarah." Robbie replied modestly.

"I don't think so, Robbie. I have always known you were

special. I just didn't say it because I was with Tom. I've always looked forward to our talks in the hallways."

Robbie felt as if this was a dream! He had fantasized about this moment since the first day he had set eyes on her. "I have always felt the same way, Sarah!"

"Thank you, Robbie," said Sarah, and reached out to touch his hand.

35

It was a typical Saturday for Tom. His mother was at work again, and he was just hanging out at home. He had been thinking through what he would say to last weekend's girl to butter her up again. She had been upset when his mom called her Sarah. He finally decided to phone her.

"Hey, Babe," he said, because he couldn't remember her name.

"What do you want?!" She was annoyed, but wanted to hear what he had to say.

"Sorry about my mom last weekend. She keeps forgetting that Sarah and I broke up months ago! I think the stress from losing my dad is taking a toll on her."

"Aw. That's understandable," her heart was softening. She was falling for it hook, line, and sinker.

"What if I take you out, as an apology? I'll pick you up in about half an hour."

Tom was feeling very proud of himself. He was able to keep two women falling in love with him and they were none the wiser. He put on some cologne and headed out to his dad's car. Along the way to pick up his date, he stopped to buy some flowers. When he presented them to her at her door, she was so touched by his kind gesture that he knew she was now under his control— she would do whatever he asked. Later, at the coffee shop, they ordered coffees and Tom did his signature move—pretending to feel for his wallet.

"Shoot. I don't have my wallet,"

"That's okay, Babe, I've got it...."

Tom couldn't believe how gullible these women could be. Sarah would be at home right now, planning their future. A future where she would look after him while he did whatever he might want to do. He had it made!

Or, so he thought...

The next day, Tom called Sarah, but she wasn't returning his calls....

36

"Well," said Jackie, "I had been dating this guy named John for about a year. We were really happy.."

"Then what happened?" Brad pulled over and stopped the car so he could give her story his full attention.

"I got pregnant!" Tears were welling up in Jackie's eyes. "I told him from the moment we found out that I wasn't ready to be a mother. I didn't even know if I wanted children at all! I told him I wanted to put the baby up for adoption, but he just wouldn't listen...kept saying things would be different once we had her, but they weren't—they were worse! He was gone all the time, and I couldn't cope!" She couldn't hold back her tears any longer.

"That's a lot! I'm sorry you had to go through all that, Jackie! "

"I understand if you just want to take me home and not talk to me anymore, Brad. I know that running away was a terrible thing! I'm a horrible person!"

"Jackie! I don't think you're horrible at all. I'm not even going to pretend to understand what that must have been like for you. I look at you and I see someone who was brave enough to speak up and say what she needed to say. You ran away because you were thrown into an impossible situation for you. You told him you weren't ready, and he didn't listen."

"Yes, that's exactly it!" Jackie looked up through her

tears, heartened to know she had been heard. "If we had given up Abigail for adoption, I would still feel guilty, but at least I would feel like we made the right decision for her. My running away leaves me questioning if I did what was best for her? I couldn't stay with John because he was pushing me into something I wasn't ready for. But...Abigail is innocent in all of this! I'm angry that he pushed me! Not that it's all his fault, but he is partly to blame for sure!" she paused for a moment. "Well, I bet this is a lot more involved than what you expected when

325

you asked what brought me
here!"

"That's for sure!" Brad
replied. "But, that's okay. We all
have a story."

37

Brad Hutchins had grown up in Vancouver with his parents Donna and Jake. They lived in an upscale neighbourhood and Brad remembered his childhood as being great. He had felt safe and cared for. His parents seemed happy and life was good, but looks can be deceiving. His mom was a real estate agent and his dad worked for a prestigious insurance company. After working his way up in the business, his dad had become

partner. Brad remembered the
excitement and celebration in
their home when that happened.
That was when Brad was twelve.
Soon after, their older domestic
cars were replaced by a
Mercedes and a BMW. Donna
continued successfully to work in
the real estate business.

It was a typical sunny day
in March. Brad was in grade 9
and had just arrived home from
school. He had his usual snack of
cookies and milk. His parents
were not home yet, but that was

usual. Around 4:30 p.m., his dad had phoned.

"Hey, Brad, is Mom home yet?" Brad could feel fear in his father's voice.

"No, not yet. Why? What's up, Dad?" Something didn't seem quite right.

"Oh, nothing, Bud, don't worry, I'll be home soon. Hey, if the phone rings again, don't answer it, okay? Oh, and pack a bag, I think it's time we take a family vacation!" And, Jake hung up.

Brad was confused by what his dad had said, and by how he said it. But, he was kind of excited at the thought of going on vacation! His parents, especially his dad, never took time off.

Just as Brad headed upstairs to pack, his dad arrived home. He yelled frantically for Brad to hurry up.

"Don't worry, Bud, we will buy new clothes when we get there! Let's just get going!"

"What about Mom?" asked Brad. He was worried now.

"We'll surprise her and pick her up on the way!" Jake was standing at the opened door of the car, motioning him to get in.

"Okay!—"Brad had barely connected his seat belt when his dad started to frantically back the car out of the driveway. But before the car had left the driveway, a police car pulled up behind it, blocking its exit. The gig was up. His dad was in some kind of trouble.

"What's going on, Dad?!" yelled Brad, confused.

Before Jake could answer, the police ordered him out of the car.

Brad was left standing at the end of his driveway with tears streaming down his face. The police were saying things to him that he couldn't comprehend. It had seemed like everything was moving in slow motion. All of sudden, he felt someone's arms around him. He looked up and saw his mom standing there hugging him. He had no idea how long she had been there. "I'm so sorry, Brad! She kept saying."

"What did he do, Mom?"

'I don't know, Honey. It must be a mistake!"

By this time, Jake's hands were cuffed and he was sitting in the back seat of the police car looking helpless.

"Don't worry, Jake!" Donna called to him. "I'll be right behind you." And then to Brad, "Go to the neighbour's. I'll come and get you as soon as I straighten this all out!"

Once she got to the police station and Jake was taken in for booking, Donna demanded answers from the officer at the desk.

"My husband, Jake Hutchins, was just brought in! What's going on?" she asked.

"Have a seat, Ma'am." Detective Collins will be right with you."

Donna sat for what seemed like hours, waiting for answers. Finally a tall, balding, hard-looking man came from one of the doors beside the front desk. He was dressed in black pants, a white shirt, and—around his neck—a lanyard that read, "Detective J. Collins" below a picture of a much younger version of himself.

"Are you Mrs. Hutchins?" he asked.

"Yes," replied Donna. She tried to steady her nerves.

"Okay, come with me." He led her through the door he had just come from.

"I'm sure there has been some kind of mistake," Donna insisted as they followed a long hallway. But there was no reply.

Finally they entered another door with a sign that read, "Interrogation Room #1."

"Have a seat, Mrs. Hutchins," Detective Collins said. "So, do you have any idea about what's happening?"

"No, not at all!" Donna replied. She felt at a loss.

"Have you noticed any sudden changes in your bank balances?"

"Nothing out of the ordinary."

"Are you aware of any other bank accounts that your husband may have had, or still has?"

"No. Not at all! What's this all about?!" *This can't be happening!*

"Your husband has been arrested for embezzlement. He has been stealing from his company."

Donna's world crumbled around her. She started to hyperventilate. The walls seemed to close in.

Detective Collins got up and opened the door.   "We need water down here!"

As she sipped the water, Donna slowly calmed herself. "How do you know that he has been doing this? What evidence is there?"

"Well, your husband's business partner was noticing discrepancies in the company's bank statements. So he started investigating and discovered that large sums of money were transferred into an offshore account. When he confronted your husband, he said that the money was for a deal that he had been working on and that it was going to be huge for the company. When asked for details about the deal, your husband's answers didn't make sense, so his partner called us in to investigate. It turns out your husband has been skimming off the top for years...to the tune of 2 million!

"How could he do this to us?" she asked. But the more she thought about it, she couldn't help but believe what he was saying.

Over the previous few years, Jake had been getting more and more materialistic—always striving for the bigger house or the faster car. "What happens to my son and me now?"

"Your husband will have a bail hearing within 24 hours. It would be a good idea for him to obtain legal counsel," Detective Collins replied.

"What do I do now? He has put his son and me in an impossible situation. Will the money I earn in *my* bank accounts be safe?" A million thoughts swirled around in her head.

"Yes, the money you earn will be safe as long as only your name is on the bank account."

"Thank goodness!" Donna sighed in relief. She had one last account that wasn't a joint account. She had been meaning to change that account, too, but fortunately she hadn't done it yet. "What should I do now?" She felt completely out of her element.

"Well, if you want to help your husband, go to his bail hearing and find him a lawyer.

What I would also suggest—to save yourself a world of hurt—is to leave this place and never look back. He has committed a crime, don't let him take you down with him!"

Donna had walked out of the police station in shock. She couldn't believe everything that she had just been told. *How could he do this to us?* She picked up Brad at her neighbour's on the way home.

"Okay, Mom," said Brad, "what's going on?"

"Your dad stole a bunch of money from work...it's not good, Brad."

Brad was devastated. His dad had been his hero!

The next day Donna and Brad had attended Jake's bail hearing. Bail was set at $25,000. Donna had no intention of letting him come back home or of paying that amount of money.

"Are we going to pay it for him, Mom?" asked Brad, wide-eyed.

"No, Honey. We don't have that kind of money anymore."

As they led him from the courtroom, Jake turned and looked at both of them with tears streaming down his face. "I'm sorry!" he mouthed to them.

Jake had been sentenced to 20 years in prison. Donna was so angry that Jake's greed had left Brad and her in such a difficult situation. Because their house and cars had been purchased with embezzled money, they were all seized. Thankfully, through Donna's real estate connections, she was quickly able to find and purchase a house across town and she bought a used Toyota to get them around. It was a huge lifestyle change, but they did what they had to do.

Haunted by the image of the tears rolling down his dad's face and struggling with the losses they had suffered in so many ways, Brad eventually turned to drugs and alcohol to numb the pain. His mom had been so busy trying to keep them afloat that she hadn't noticed the signs at first. He started having a few drinks and smoking some weed. Then, one night at a party, he tried coke for the first time. He had never felt so free. Unfortunately, as good as the highs may have seemed, the lows were ten times worse. Donna was starting to see a change in him. He was moody and always needing money. She would question him about what he was up to, but he would just say that he was hanging out with his friends, or getting some food.

Finally, after one year of living this way and making a lot of bad choices, Brad had admitted to his mother that he had a drug problem. Donna made some calls and got him into a rehab facility in the next city. He spent three months there and came out clean and determined to stay that way. He attended counselling and continued clean. It had been two years: one year on drugs and alcohol, and another year becoming drug-free and alcohol-free. *This* freedom was the best!

Brad had returned to school, excelling in his studies, surrounding himself with a good crowd, and planning his future.

38

"Did you hear anything from John? Is he coming today?" Rebecca asked Robbie at the next church service.

"No, I didn't hear anything. Hopefully, next week he will," replied Robbie. "He seems like a really great guy—" Robbie smiled and teasingly poked her, "—you like John!"

"No, I don't." Rebecca blushed. "It was fun hanging out with him though, and Abigail is so adorable! Yes, it *was* a really good night!"

It was later that afternoon, when Robbie was just relaxing on the couch, that the phone rang. He fully expected it to be Rebecca wanting to plan what they might do later. But it was Sarah's voice and she sounded really upset as she explained through her tears. *That idiot, Tom, has really done it this time!* "Mom, I have to go! I won't be late!"

When Robbie arrived at the coffee shop it took all the

restraint he had to keep from
going in and wiping that smug
grin off Tom's face. How could
Tom cheat on Sarah? Seeing her
this upset, broke Robbie's heart.
Maybe now she was seeing the
light about Tom. Robbie felt
honoured that she had called
him.

They drove around for a
while talking. "How was I so
stupid?" Sarah asked Robbie with
tears running down her face.

"You aren't stupid, Sarah!
Tom knows how to play people
with kind hearts like you! He's an

expert at taking advantage.
You've always been so sweet."

They finally stopped at a
little restaurant that they both
liked. They went in and ate,
talked, laughed, and cried. They
truly enjoyed each other's
company. Sarah told Robbie
some deeply personal things that
she had never been comfortable
talking about before. Robbie just
listened with no judgement.

"We all make mistakes..."
he said.

"To be honest, Robbie, I
have been falling for you for

months! But then, Tom's dad died and I didn't feel that I could leave him. Plus, I—uh—I didn't know if you would want me at all after I had been with Tom." *There! I said it.* Sarah couldn't believe she had just blurted that out.

Robbie looked deeply into her eyes and gently took her hand. "Sarah, honestly, I have loved you since the moment I first saw you. I don't care about the mistakes you have made! God's mercies are new every morning and you are no more a sinner than I am!"

Sarah leaned over the table—with new, happier tears this time streaming down her face—and kissed him. Robbie was on Cloud 9! They talked about their future plans. Sarah thought it awesome that Robbie still wanted to be a youth pastor. Now that he had two approval letters, it was very real. Sarah was hoping that he would choose the college closer to the Niagara area, but she decided not to say anything—he needed to do what was best for him. Little did she know that—right then and there—Robbie had decided that he would be sticking around!

Sarah told Robbie about her parents and how they were considering making her a partner in the family business, about the argument she had had with them over Tom, and how guilty she felt about the argument. "I need to apologize, but I'm just not ready to face them right now," she said.

"What if I come with you?" Robbie offered.

"You would do that?"

"I'd do anything for you, Sarah."

39

John had really enjoyed hanging out with Robbie and Rebecca at the coffee shop. It was just so easy to be around them. They didn't have a look of pity on their faces, and they didn't seem to judge him. They just treated him like a normal person. He had found himself smiling and laughing for the first time since Jackie left. They actually made him forget his heartache for a while. And, of course, Rebecca was incredible! The fact that she was able to comfort Abigail was so touching to him. He didn't want to fall for anyone else—not yet—but it was happening.

John saw Robbie at school the next Monday. "Hey Robbie!" he called.

"Hey John! How was the rest of your weekend?"

"Really good. Abigail and I just hung out with my parents. How about you?"

"My weekend was amazing!" replied Robbie still in

shock over the turn of events with Sarah.

"Oh ya? How come?" asked John, intrigued.

"I'll fill you in later, but...Sarah and I are together now!" Robbie was bursting with excitement.

"Really? That's awesome!" John gave Robbie a high-five. John was happy for them both— two good people finally caught a break! John was also feeling happy because he had been afraid that something might have been developing between Robbie and Rebecca, but now Robbie

had put those fears to rest. "Hey,

um...Rebecca seems really cool..."

John said a bit shyly.

Robbie smiled, "She said

the same about you. Do you want

her phone number?"

"Yes!" John blushed at

how quickly he replied.

That afternoon, when John

got home from school, he gave

Rebecca a call.

"Hello? Oh, hello John."

"Hey Rebecca, I hope you don't mind but I got your number from Robbie."

""Not at all, I'm glad you called!" replied Rebecca. *I need to remember to thank Robbie*, she thought.

"I really enjoyed meeting you on Saturday," said John.

"I enjoyed meeting you, too! You *and* Abigail."

"I was wondering if you'd like to go out for dinner tomorrow night?" John ventured.

"Sounds good to me! Thanks, John."

And they made their plans.

Early evening the next day, with flowers in hand, John picked up Rebecca and they headed to the restaurant.

"You look beautiful, Rebecca."

"Thanks!" It was Rebecca's turn to blush.

Soon they were talking as if they had known each other their whole lives.

Rebecca told Robbie all about how she was adopted and how she had struggled with dyslexia throughout her life. John told her all about his upbringing. He talked about his mom's multiple sclerosis and how it had affected his family. He also talked about his dad's business and how he was planning on following in his footsteps. Rebecca was so pleasantly surprised at how easy it was to talk with John. He wasn't like other guys that only half-listened. She knew that she had John's full attention when she spoke.

Then, of course, they talked about Jackie and Abigail. John told Rebecca how devastated he was after Jackie left. "It felt as if someone had ripped the stuffing out of me. I felt like I didn't have the strength to carry on. But then I would look over at Abigail lying in her bassinet and I just knew I had to pick myself up. I had no choice!

"I would imagine that my parents might understand a little part of that from their experience adopting me," replied Rebecca, trying to relate.

"Yes, that's a very good point! I'd love to talk with them about it sometime, if they wouldn't mind?"

"They'd love that!" Rebecca replied. "You know, as soon as Robbie heard about what you were going through, we were both praying for you. I don't know what you believe, but I know that God has been with you."

"I didn't really know what it was, but I felt this strange sense of peace that seemed to come out of nowhere...was that God?" asked John.

"Yes, John, he does that for us. He loves you and Abigail totally."

"Wow! I really want to learn more. I think I'm going to take you up on your offer and come to church with you on Sunday.

"That would be wonderful," replied Rebecca, falling more and more in love with this young man.

40

Jackie sat with bated breath while she listened to Brad tell her his story.

"Did you ever want to visit your dad?" Jackie asked.

"Yes, I wanted to, but Mom wouldn't allow it. She was always very angry. I think that was part of my problem all these years. She was trying to protect me in her own way, but I didn't see that." But then he added, with some bitterness, "It's not like he ever reached out to me." And then, with a half-hearted chuckle, "You can tell I had to go through a ton of counselling!"

"That's totally understandable. Did you feel abandoned by him?" Jackie was obviously talking about more than just Brad's situation.

"I did at times," he admitted. "I was angry that he chose to do these things that could mean that he'd have to leave us."

"Ya, I can see that. I wonder if that's how Abigail will

feel without me." She was starting to wonder if she should try to have some kind of contact with Abigail.

"Do you want to be a part of her life?"

"I really don't want her growing up thinking I didn't love her. I left because of the pressure everyone was putting on me, not because I didn't love her! "Jackie started to cry.

"Maybe one day we could go to Niagara Falls and visit her?"

Jackie looked over at him in surprise. "You would come with me?" she asked.

"Yes, I'd love to travel and spend more time with you!" he said with that big goofy smile Jackie was beginning to love.

"Maybe someday," Jackie replied. They were silent for a few minutes while Jackie got lost in thought. *I wonder how big Abigail is now. I wonder if she is starting to roll over....*

Then Brad broke the silence with a change in the subject. "So, what do you think of prom and graduation? They're only a month away. Do you think maybe you'd like to go with me?"

"Definitely." Jackie was smiling. Even though she hadn't known him long, she could tell that Brad was different. She definitely wanted to get to know him better. She had a little pang of guilt talking about prom because she and John had talked about nothing else before she got pregnant. But—as they say—a baby changes everything.

They continued to drive around and talk until, finally, they checked the time.

"Wow, it's getting late!"

"Well, as they say, time flies when you're having fun!" Jackie laughed.

"I think we need to head home, eh?"

When they got back home, Brad walked Jackie to her door. "I had a really good time. Thanks for trusting me with your story, Jackie. I know it wasn't easy for you to open up."

"Thank you for listening and also sharing *your* story," replied Jackie.

"Let's do this again soon," Brad said as he leaned in to give her a kiss on the cheek. "See you tomorrow!" he yelled out the car window as he drove into his own driveway next door.

"Yes, you will," Jackie called back.

When Jackie closed the door, her aunt was there waiting for her. "Where have you been?"

"I went for a drive with Brad. Sorry, Aunt Jane, I should have left a note."

"Yes, you should have, I was worried sick!"

Jackie had never seen her like this. "I'm very, very sorry, Aunt Jane!"

"It's okay. Just don't go out like that again without telling me, okay?"

"I won't," promised Jackie and she headed to her bedroom to get some homework done. Jackie thought about everything she and Brad had talked about. She couldn't believe that she had opened up to him so easily. *What was I thinking? I barely know the guy! What am I doing having feelings for him, too?! Haven't I learned anything from my experience with John?!* Jackie was so confused. She felt that maybe leaving Abigail had been a bad decision. Maybe she could have just left John and his mother but still kept a relationship with her daughter. Ugh! It was so hard to know what to do. Then Brad had offered to go to Niagara Falls with her. *First things first! First I'm*

going to finish high school; then
I'll figure the rest out later.

The months flew by. Brad and Jackie went to prom together and graduated with their classmates and friends. Brad hadn't breathed a word about Jackie's past to anyone, even though she hadn't asked him to keep it confidential. Jackie was so thankful that he respected her privacy and kept it between them. Their relationship was blossoming into something neither one of them was expecting. All of Brad's friends and of course his cousin,

Jennifer, liked Jackie and enjoyed

hanging out with the new couple.

Jackie and Brad did everything

together.

Before they knew it, a year

had gone by and they were both

immersed in their college

courses—at the same college.

Things were moving in the right

direction. Jackie still thought a lot

about Abigail and wondered what

the future would hold. She would

talk to Sarah every so often and

get an update on what Abigail

was doing now. She was so

happy that Sarah had finally left Tom. She didn't know Robbie that well, but he seemed nice. Jackie wondered if she would ever go back to visit Abigail. Sometimes she wanted to.

One Sunday afternoon a call came for Jackie. She had to sit to process what she was hearing.

"What's going on Jackie? Who was that?" Aunt Jane was immediately concerned about the distress on Jackie's face.

It took Jackie a minute to find the words. It all seemed so

surreal. "It...was the hospital in Niagara Falls. M-Mom was in an accident...sh-sh-she didn't make it!" After her thoughts and emotions stopped spinning, her maternal instinct kicked in and she knew she needed to call John and make sure that Abigail would hear the news from him and not someone else. The thought of her little girl losing someone else in her life broke Jackie's heart. She knew right then that she wanted to have some kind of relationship with Abigail. She obviously cared about her, but she still just couldn't picture how that

relationship could be.

41

That night after Sarah left Tom, and she and Robbie had shared their feelings toward each other, Robbie took Sarah home to face her parents. She had been gone for hours and they knew that her parents would be worried.

"Are you sure about this?" asked Sarah as they pulled into her driveway.

"Yes, Sarah, I want to be there for you. Let's do this!"

"Okay, here goes," she said getting out of the car.

As soon as they walked through the door, Jen appeared with open arms. Greg was close behind.

"I've been so worried about you!" she cried and gave Sarah a long, tight hug.

"I know, Mom. I'm sorry," replied Sarah. "This is Robbie James. Let's sit down, Mom, Dad. We have a lot to talk about."

Sarah and Robbie filled them in on the night's events.

"Oh Sarah, I'm so sorry," said her mom, trying very hard not to say, *I told you so*.

"I know you guys said he was a loser, but I just didn't want to see it. Even Robbie tried to warn me," she said and Robbie nodded.

"So, is Tom officially gone now?" asked Greg.

"Yes, Dad, I'm done with him."

"Amen to that! But don't jump too fast into anything else either!"

"Yes, Dad, I know." Sarah said and turned toward Robbie with a huge smile on her face. "But Robbie is the complete opposite of Tom. We'll see what happens."

Jen and Greg looked at each other nervously. They really hoped she was not jumping into another bad relationship. Only time would tell.

Sarah had been avoiding Tom's calls and dodging him at school. She really didn't feel like she owed him any explanation and she was afraid of what she might do if she talked to him again. She didn't want to give him any more chances. She had finally met a real man. Robbie was so sweet and he treated her like a queen! She had hoped that things would be okay for Robbie once Tom knew that Robbie had replaced him. She didn't want any trouble. Tom could be a hot head, so she and Robbie were keeping it to themselves until prom. Only a month to go!

At school, Tom finally caught up to Sarah in the hallway. "Hey, Babe, what's going on? You've been a hard person to get a hold of!" he said.

"Yes, well, you're not who I thought you were, Tom." Sarah could feel her anger suddenly rising.

"What's that supposed to mean?" Tom was completely clueless, as usual.

"Tom, I saw you at the coffee shop with that girl on Saturday."

"Oh!"

"Really, Tom? That's all you've got? How long has this

been going on?!" She yelled, unable to hold back anymore.

"Well, I told you I needed my time! She's just a friend, Sarah."

"Ya! A friend that you kiss, eh? No, I don't think so, Tom!" This was becoming a scene in the hallway.

At that moment, Robbie sauntered by—he didn't want to make it obvious, but wanted to make sure Sarah was okay. "Sarah? Tom? What's going on?"

"Robbie!" Sarah ran over to him. "Tom was wondering why I've been avoiding him..."

"Ah, yes. I bet he was," replied Robbie. He was struggling against expressing   words and emotions that he knew he would regret later. "What did you tell him?"

Tom shifted from one foot to the other. "She says she saw me with another chick. That was just a friend."

"Can I explain it to him, Sarah?" and with her nod, Robbie proceeded to do so. "Well, Tom,

Sarah saw you with that other "chick," as you put It. She saw you through the window of the coffee shop after she had just finished defending you in a big argument with her parents...about YOU!! She had gone to the payphone to call you. When your mom said you were out, Sarah turned her head and there you were—making out in the coffee shop with another girlfriend!"

"Whatever! You guys have probably had a thing for each other this whole time, anyway!" Tom yelled back.

"Tom, you know that's not true!" Sarah shouted through tears of anger. "You know I did everything I could for you! It's you that ruined this! Not us!"

Robbie came over to Sarah and gave her a big hug and a kiss.

"Ha-ha-ha! You two deserve each other! Thanks for being such a good friend, Robbie!" Tom's voice dripped with bitterness and sarcasm. Then he turned and left.

The murmuring group of on-lookers cheered, then quickly

dissipated—the show was over.

Sarah and Robbie walked away

hand in hand. No need to hide

anymore.

42

Tom was fuming when he walked away. *How dare she humiliate me like that! And Robbie! What kind of friend was he?! Doesn't he know that you don't break the 'bro code' with another guy's girl?!*

"Whatever," muttered Tom under his breath. He didn't need them anyway.

When Tom got home that night, his mother was waiting for

him. "Tom, have you found a job yet?" she asked.

"Oh, Mom! Seriously, this again?"

"Yes, this again. I told you that if you didn't start contributing soon, you'd be out!"

"So what are you saying, Mom?! You're kicking me out?!"

"Not exactly," she said, "but you're going to start paying rent. The rest of this month will be free so that you can find a job and get your first pay cheque. But after that you can pay me $500 a month." Carole felt proud of herself for finally getting a backbone.

"What?! Ugh! Whatever!" and Tom stormed off.

Tom created a resume the next day and started handing out copies after school. He quickly realized that aside from wooing girls, he hadn't developed skills. He started applying everywhere. Finally, after a few days, he got a call from the coffee shop. He hated the thought of having to work where he and his friends hung out together, but he had no choice, no one else would hire him.

Tom had his first shift a few days later and was humiliated when he put the uniform on. He had to wear a visor and a pink and black apron. He was the most recently hired so he had to clean the washrooms, sweep the floors, and make the coffee. Everyone employed there had to do those things, but they loved passing off their jobs to the new guy who didn't know any better. As it turned out, he had to work alongside his ex-girlfriend,

Joanna! *Great, he thought, as if this could get any worse!*

"Hey, Tom, are you actually going to keep this job and be faithful to it? Or are you going to move on to a better coffee shop?! asked Joanna sarcastically.

"Is this what I'm in for every time we have to work together?!"

"Well, Tom, you did use me...and cheat on me!" After a moment, her expression changed to sadness. "But I was sorry to hear about your dad." Right then

Tom knew he was winning her over.

"Thank you." He hung his head to show just enough heartache to make her feel bad for him. His dad would be proud!

Tom got used to his friends' relentless teasing when they would come in for a coffee. Joanna was quickly falling for him again, so he didn't mind working weekends as much as he thought he would. His mother was happy that he was working and he was happy to be able to continue living at home.

Sarah and Robbie had come into the coffee shop a couple of times, but Tom didn't care. It was Sarah's problem, not his! And what was up with Robbie? How could he betray Tom like that? *Oh well, their loss*, he thought.

Tom asked Joanna to the prom and, of course, she went with him. Tom took his dad's Mustang and picked up Joanna. She looked lovely with her blonde hair and blue eyes, and dressed in a long black dress with a slit up the side. She was almost as tall

as Tom. Tom was dressed in a
rented black tux that his mom had
paid for. He had brought a flask
full of whiskey to make the party
more interesting later. They drove
to the banquet hall where the
prom was being held. It was
buzzing with excitement and
beautifully decorated. Tom sized
up the crowd and decided that he
had landed the hottest chick in
the room...until Sarah and Robbie
showed up. Sarah glowed in her
long red dress with spaghetti
straps and sweetheart neckline;
Robbie handsomely sported a
black suit with red tie. Tom

399

cringed with jealousy when he saw how in-love they looked. Sarah used to look at him that way!

When no one was looking, Tom pulled out his flask and took a big swig of the whisky to calm his nerves. He hated feeling this way. Joanna was none the wiser, dancing and having a great time.

"Let's go!" Tom demanded.

"Why? We just got here." Joanna was puzzled.

"We're leaving!" he said, grabbing her by the arm.

"No, I don't want to go yet!
Stop, Tom, your hurting me! Have
you been drinking?"

That caught Sarah and
Robbie's attention. They hurried
over.

"What's going on?!" yelled
Sarah over all the commotion.

"Oh, great! You guys!"
Tom took another drink from his
flask. He was not even trying to
hide it now. "Joanna, let's go!
Now!" he shouted again.

"She doesn't need to go
anywhere with you! Especially in

your condition!" Robbie edged

between Tom and Joanna.

"Oh, just move, Robbie! Are you trying to take another girlfriend away from me?!" Tom's words were beginning to slur.

Sarah watched in disbelief. *How could Tom stoop so low!*

By this point Joanna was crying so Sarah reached out to console her. "So you're the Sarah he was dating before?" Joanna asked.

"Yes, that's me."

"That explains why he wanted to leave so soon, I guess."

"Yes, I guess he has a guilty conscience," Sarah agreed.

"He told me you just up and left him for his best friend," said Joanna.

"Well, that's partially true. But that was only after I saw him making out with another girl in the coffee shop! He had treated me like garbage the whole time we were together! It took Robbie's helping me for me to see how a real man treats a lady! Believe me, you can do way better!"

Joanna felt so stupid. "I was with him before...I'm Joanna Turner...did you know about what happened between us before?" Joanna asked with embarrassment.

"Yes, I heard—that was before I started dating him, but I didn't want to believe it. He is a very charming guy. Please don't feel embarrassed. He knows how to make us fall for every word he says."

"Thanks for saying that, Sarah. I feel like such a fool."

"No. You're not a fool at all! You're a good person and that's why you felt bad for him." Sarah replied as she reached into her purse and handed Joanna a tissue.

"Thanks, Sarah."

Meanwhile, Robbie was trying to get Tom calmed down. He didn't want Tom to storm off and drive away. He was obviously drunk by now.

"Tom, let's talk about this."
Robbie tried to reason with him.

"What's there to talk
about? You stole my girlfriend
and betrayed me!" yelled Tom,
flailing his arms around and trying
to stumble to the door.

"Okay, come on, Buddy.
We have been friends for a long
time! We have always been able
to talk. I've always been the one
sitting back listening to you talk
about all the girls in your life—
about all the times you got away
with having one girlfriend and
another on the side. You have

406

always been so proud of that! It's not right, Tom. You can't expect a young woman like Sarah or your date tonight to put up with that forever! They are worth more than that!"

"Whatever!!" yelled Tom, then ran out to his car and sped away.

"Call the police." Robbie called over to Sarah. "He's going to kill someone or himself." And Sarah and Joanna ran to find a phone to call 911.

Tom was soon apprehended and taken to jail for

underage drinking and for driving while intoxicated.

Sarah felt sad for Tom's mother. She called Carole to fill her in on what had happened and could hear the devastation in her voice.

"I wish he hadn't ruined things with you, Sarah! But, this might be the wake-up call that he needs. Thanks, Sarah."

"I know that it wouldn't have worked out. Take care, Mrs. Brown." Sarah replied and slowly hung up the phone.

"Do you want us to take you home, Joanna?" asked Sarah.

"No, I think I'll just call my dad. I think I just need to be alone for a bit. Thanks, though."

'Okay," Sarah fully understood how Joanna was feeling.

43

"Can I pick you up for church in the morning?" John asked.

"That would be great!" Rebecca replied. They had been going to church together for a while now. John and Abigail loved it there, too. After church, they would all hang out with Robbie's family at Arby's restaurant. Sometimes Rebecca's family would join them. They all loved John and Abigail and the people

John was surrounded with were helping him come to terms with his situation. Abigail loved Rebecca, as did John, and he became comfortable with bringing Abigail to Rebecca's home. Their discussions would sometimes turn toward Jackie's leaving, John's and her divorce, and how he was managing everything. Rebecca's parents always gave him their loving Christian perspective. He usually left there feeling uplifted and they were gaining respect for him.

John would come home and tell his parents all about the great people he had met and the uplifting messages the pastor had preached. They thought that he was just being a lost teenager looking to escape reality. He kept going anyway.

John had fallen very much in love with Rebecca. Now that his and Jackie's divorce was finalized, there was nothing stopping him from proposing to Rebecca. He'd ask her parents for their blessing then...maybe on the night of the prom...ask her to marry him. He told Robbie and

Sarah his plan and they were

beyond excited. John's parents

loved Rebecca too, and they

knew that—even though John and

Rebecca were young—the life

they had planned for John had

already taken a different direction

from their earliest dreams for him.

Getting married now made sense,

then their future—further

education, careers, more

children, whatever they wanted—

was theirs to create together.

John picked out a beautiful

diamond engagement ring and on

the night of the prom would tuck it

safely into his pocket. He was worried that–maybe–she wouldn't say *yes*, and decided to let the night dictate when the timing felt right to ask her. He had asked his friends to keep this a secret as he still didn't know when during the evening he was going to pop the question.

Robbie picked up Rebecca at her home and it was like a scene from a movie. She looked stunning. Her face lit up when she saw him and his heart melted. She was wearing the beautiful black floor length dress

414

with brown overlay. Her curly hair was in an up-do with wisps of curls.

"Wow! You look amazing, Rebecca!" Robbie managed to say.

"Thank you. And you look very handsome!"

Robbie and Rebecca had a great night dancing and laughing with Sarah and Robbie. A slow song that Robbie and Rebecca both loved began as they were sitting at their table, taking a break from dancing.

"Come on, John! We *have* to dance to this one!" Rebecca grabbed John's hand and turned toward the dance floor.

"Wait!" he called over the music. When Rebecca turned back to look at him, he was down on one knee. "Rebecca, I love you very much. You make Abigail and me very happy—"

By now, a few people were starting to notice what was happening and that only made John more nervous. Rebecca's hand flew to her mouth—she couldn't believe what was happening.

"–Rebecca, I can't imagine a life without you in it. I promise I will encourage you and be your biggest fan…" John continued, fumbling in his pocket for the ring. "It's gone! It must have fallen out on the dance floor! Everybody stop!"

The music stopped. The lights suddenly filled the room. And everyone started searching for the ring. "Found it!" Someone called and brought it over to John.

"Thank you!" John gave a sigh of relief, turned to Rebecca, and with a laugh sank to his knee again. "Well, I guess by now you've figured out what I was getting at—"

"—Yes! Yes! The answer is yes! Stand up, John." Rebecca exclaimed.

John slipped the ring on her finger and, in unison, they said "I love you!" then kissed.

Everyone congratulated them and the party continued for a couple hours more.

Sarah and Robbie hugged them both, and over the sounds of the music and excitement around them, shouted that they could hardly wait to attend their wedding.

The following May, John and Rebecca were married in their church. It was a small affair of only family and a few close friends. Abigail, who was now 2 years old and walking, was their flower girl. The ceremony was touching and memorable. One of the wedding presents was a week at a cottage in Northern Ontario, so the new family of three gladly headed there the day after the wedding.

John and Rebecca had been saving up all year for a home of their own. John had been working really hard at his dad's business and had been able to save up a down payment. Rebecca had accepted a position at their church as the director of the children's ministry. The home they found was perfect with a greenery-edged yard for Abigail to play in. Life was good. Along with John and Rebecca, Abigail had their parents and Jackie's mother—lots of grandparents— around her who adored her and, John hoped, maybe that made up for Jackie's absence. Until he received a phone call that would change everything.

44

It was a Sunday afternoon when John's phone rang. He, Rebecca, and Abigail had just returned from a walk.

"Hello," John said.

"Hi, John. It's J—"

"Jackie!"

"Ya, I thought I should call...I didn't know if you had heard yet..." Jackie's voice trembled.

"Heard what?"

"It's my mom, John, she—
she's gone!"

John grabbed a chair.
Jackie's voice was the first shock,
but now to hear that her mom
was gone... "What happened?"

"She was in a car
accident—earlier this morning.
She—died this afternoon!"

"Oh, no!! I'm so sorry,
Jackie!!" He had become fond of
Barb as a valued part of his,
Rebecca's and Abigail's circle.
And he was sorry that—for Abigail,
especially— this would be yet

another loss in her family.
Another loss!!

"Thanks, John. I just
wanted Abigail and you to know
before you hear it from someone
else. "

"Oh, *now* you are
concerned for Abigail, eh?" John
retorted.

"Yes, I know how it must
sound, John, and you have every
right to say that. But there's
something else…my mom left the
house to me. I think I'm moving
back, John, and I might be ready
to be in Abigail's life…"

John was seeing red! He couldn't believe what he was hearing! How dare she decide to walk back into their lives after all this time. She had no idea how hard it had been for him to pick up the pieces after she left! He was stuck raising Abigail all on his own! Now that he finally had found someone who was a wonderful mother to Abigail, all of a sudden Jackie wanted to come back. This was all too much!

"I'm really very sorry for your loss, Jackie. We will all miss her very much. *Very* much. But...I have to go!" He said and hung up.

He sat in the kitchen for a few minutes taking in all that he had just heard. His mind was racing. How was he going to tell Abigail all of this news? Or any of it? She was too young to understand, yet big changes would be happening to her life. She had screamed for mommy for a few months after Jackie left, but she eventually stopped. Now she was calling Rebecca *mommy*. What was this going to do to her? Then there was Rebecca.

After their marriage, Rebecca had slipped into the mothering role so flawlessly. It just seemed to happen naturally and John was so relieved to see Abigail thriving. And he, himself, finally felt settled and genuinely happy. What was this going to do to his family? Then there was his mom who had never stopped bad mouthing Jackie for leaving. *This will add fuel to the fire*, he thought.

45

Jackie and Aunt Jane had received the news in shock when the phone call came.

"When?" Jane then asked, as tears came to her eyes.

"She died...this afternoon, Aunt Jane. Mom...died! They said the accident happened this morning!" After a few moments, Jackie said, "I need to call John so he can tell Abigail. And we—or I—will need to go and make the arrangements for Mom in Niagara Falls."

"Yes. That's a big responsibility, Jackie. We'll do this together. I can't believe we've lost Barb...and in such...a...horrible way!!"

Jackie called Brad and asked him to come over. She didn't want to do this over the phone.

"Sure. I'll be right there," Brad said, and rushed over.

Jackie and Jane filled Brad in on the sad news and their travel plans.

"This means I'll have to leave, Brad. I have no idea when I might get back to Vancouver, "Jackie said.

Brad was taken aback. He stood thinking in silence for a few moments. "Well, I'll come with you," he responded.

"Really?!"

"Well, what's the other option? I don't want to lose you, and I'm sure you'll need support going through all of this. Plus, I'd miss you if I didn't come—"

"What do you think your mom will say?" Jackie asked.

"Bye!" Brad grinned. His mother had recently met a man and was finally happy again. "She doesn't need me hanging around here anymore. And flights between here and there are quick and easy."

It was settled. Brad went home to tell his mother. She took the news just as he expected-- gave him a big hug and told him how much she loved him. She made him promise to call as soon as they reached Niagara Falls, and to stay in touch as his plans developed, reminding him that they can still visit back and forth. Then he started packing.

"Mom, do you know where my passport and birth certificate are?" Brad called.

Yes, they're in the middle drawer of the filing cabinet," she replied. His mom was very organized. Her motto: *a place for everything and everything in its place*.

Brad went down to his mom's office in the basement. It always smelled of scented candles and faint traces of the perfume she would wear while she worked. He opened the second drawer of the 4-drawer metal filing cabinet and quickly found his passport and birth certificate. As he closed the drawer, the muffled thud of something dropping came from behind the drawer. Puzzled, Brad pulled the drawer all the way out, reached to the back, and pulled out a big stack of letters with an elastic band around them. They had his dad's hand writing on them and were addressed to Brad! Jake had been sending his son letters all these years from prison, and Brad hadn't seen them before this!

His thoughts spun as he quickly opened the letters one after the other. In them, Jake had said how sorry he was. He had written about how much he missed Brad and Brad's mom. The latest letters talked about how he was helping other people in jail, teaching them business skills and being a mentor. He said how much he had wished that he could have been that to Brad. Brad read all these things with tears rolling down his face. How could his mother have kept all this from him?! He knew that she was angry with his dad, but why did she punish Brad? He was still Brad's father! Just then his mother came down the stairs.

"Did you fi–" she started, then froze.

"Oh ya! I found some things, Mom! How could you keep these from me? All these years, I thought he left us and forgot about us. All the times I cried to you that I didn't understand! You just kept telling me that he left us and that it would be better if I just forgot about him! None of that was true at all! I still could have talked to him and got my own closure from all of this. You took that from me! I'll never forgive you for this!" He frantically raced back upstairs and threw the rest of his things into his bags, while his mother followed, sobbing.

"Please, Brad! Please listen to me! You have to understand why I did it. I didn't want you to be manipulated by him. Please let me explain!" She cried.

"I can't do this with you right now," Brad replied in an eerily calm voice. "I'm leaving now. You take care of yourself, okay, Mom?" And with that, he was gone. Donna was left sobbing in a heap on the floor.

Brad made his way over to Jackie's house with all his travel bags, ready to leave and never look back. But there was one thing he needed to do before they left. He wanted to visit his father and he needed to do it now—alone.

Their flight was to leave at midnight. Brad looked at his watch: it was 5:00 p.m.

"There's something I really need to do before we go, Jackie. I'll be back in a couple hours and I'll fill you in then, okay?" he said.

"Okay," replied a bewildered Jackie. She was hoping that he wasn't changing his mind about coming with her.

46

The jail was about half an hour away from Jackie's house. Brad would have plenty of time to get there and back before they would have to leave. As he drove he became more and more nervous. He wondered what it would be like to see his dad after all these years. When Brad arrived at the jail, he went in and asked to visit his father.

"Do you have a visiting order?" asked the woman behind the desk.

"No, I don't. I just found out that he has been writing letters to me for years and my mom was keeping them from me! I'm leaving tonight for Niagara Falls and I was just hoping I could come in and see him before I have to leave."

"Well...we aren't allowed to do this, but as your dad has been a model inmate, I'll allow it," the woman said.

"Thank you so much!" Brad replied.

After he was patted down and the guards were sure that he

had no weapons, Brad was brought to the visitors' waiting room. His palms were sweaty; he had no idea what to expect. "Hutchins," he heard a voice say, "you have a visitor." Then he heard footsteps coming toward the door. With a loud click, the door opened and there—in front of him—was his dad and a correctional officer.

Jake had aged quite a bit since Brad had last seen him. It was strange to see him in prison clothes. In the last memories

Brad had of his dad, he was always wearing a suit and tie.

"Brad?!" His dad couldn't believe what he was seeing.

"Ya, it's me, Dad," Brad replied. "Wow! Can I hug him?" he asked the correctional officer.

"Yes, go ahead."

"It's so good to see you!" Jake said, giving his son a long, tight hug.

"You too, Dad! I'm sorry it's taken me so long to get here. I just found your letters today. I thought you had forgotten about me. Now I know that's not true!"

"No, I never forgot about you, Brad! Everything I ever did was for you and your mom!"

"What do you mean?" Brad stepped back, dumbfounded. "How could all of this have been for us?!"

"Well, I wanted to give you guys the life you wanted. The more money I made, the more things we had—nicer house, better cars. You always had the newest toys..."

"You really think we got the life we wanted?! Mom was always so stressed out! We had to move! They repossessed the house and cars! I ended up in rehab!" yelled Brad. He could no longer contain his emotions.

"Son, I had no idea what happened after I got arrested. Your mother wouldn't talk to me! It's not like I asked for any of this either!"

"Oh ya! So now it's all Mom's fault?! Wow, Dad, you are exactly what Mom said you were— a selfish jerk! You were never

444

around, even when you weren't in jail! I just came to see you today to tell you that I found your letters, but I don't care! You did this all for yourself. Gave up on me, left me without a father—all for yourself.! Well, I'm leaving Vancouver now. I may even move away, and now you can know what it feels like to be abandoned!" Brad called for the guard. "I'm done here, guard. Can you please let me out?"

"Brad, wait! Let's talk about this!" his dad called. But

Brad was already out the door, heading for the parking lot.

The drive back to Jackie's was very emotional for him. He was feeling emotions come up that he thought he had dealt with. Things he thought he was done with were coming back up to the surface. For the first time in a year, he had that all too familiar craving for some white powder in his nose. He knew where he could easily get some, too. The thought was so tempting. That had been his refuge so many times before when times got hard. He didn't like the way he felt when he had to deal with raw emotions. He would always quiet them with chemicals. That sudden rush of the feeling of weightlessness and contentment was tempting, even though he always knew that the landing would hurt more and more every time. Then he thought of Jackie. They were building something stable. Something that made him want to do better and to be a man. He needed her as much as she needed him. He needed to stop somewhere and call his sponsor before he ended up

running to his dealer.

47

Back at Brad's home, his mother was frantic. She ran over to talk to Jane and Jackie.

After expressing her condolences, Donna asked, "Have you seen Brad?!" She looked at Jackie hopefully through tear-filled eyes.

"Yes, Mrs. Hutchins. He was here for a few minutes, but then he said there was something that he had to do. He told me he would be back well before the time we need to leave to catch our flight. Why? What's going on?" Jackie's concern was mounting quickly.

"Come in, Donna. I'll make us all a cup of tea." Aunt Jane piped up.

As Donna sipped her camomile tea, she filled them in on what had happened. She told them everything about their family's story. Brad had already told Jackie much of it, but she didn't know anything had happened earlier that day.

"He was so calm when he was here, Donna," Jackie said, worried. "I didn't pick up on anything unusual..."

"Where do you think he went? Are you thinking the same thing I am? I certainly hope not! I really don't think that selfish idiot we call his father is going to give him what he "needs"! If so, Brad will be left the same way Jake always leaves people...sad, angry, and alone." Donna's hands trembled as she placed the tea cup carefully back on its saucer.

"Well, hopefully you're wrong, and things are fine. Maybe they are just catching up on the last 20 years!" Jackie replied, trying to feel optimistic.

"I thought I was protecting him from a world of hurt by not showing him those letters," Donna sobbed. "It was hard to know what to do."

"You clearly did what you did out of love. You did what you thought was right. This was not done with the intention of hurting him," Aunt Jane reassured. "But I just have one question: Why

452

didn't you simply throw out the letters?"

There was silence.

"I'm not sure," Donna finally replied. "I tried to throw them out a couple of times but couldn't bring myself to do it. I guess I had some kind of remorse for not telling Brad...I don't know...it's all just such a mess!"

"What you and Brad have been through is beyond terrible, Donna!" Aunt Jane refilled their cups. "I honestly don't know what I would have done in your situation. I'm so sorry for what you have all gone through."

By now, all three of them were wiping away their tears. What agony! All they could do was to wait and pray for him to come back to them. They all had the same fear that he might turn to drugs again. Jackie didn't know what she would do if that happened. He might need help that she couldn't offer. She loved him but she might be in over her head...again. Then she gave herself a shake—what a horrible way to think! Giving up on a guy like that! Her mind was all over the place. First, one real loss today; now, another possible loss!

Jackie kept looking at the time. It was 7:00 pm, then 8:00, 8:30...9....was he coming back? Was he going to come to Niagara Falls with them and start their lives together there?

48

"Michael, It's Brad!"

"Hey, Brad! How are you doing? Are you okay?" Michael, Brad's sponsor, hadn't heard from him for quite a while.

"Well, not great. It's been a really bad day." Brad started to get emotional.

"Where are you? Are you safe?" Michael asked.

"Yes, I'm at a payphone outside a store. Nowhere near my dealer."

"Oh, good. Tell me what happened today," Michael replied in a soft, caring voice.

"Well, my girlfriend's mother died, so we are flying to Niagara Falls tonight. If all goes well there, we may stay and start a new life together. She has a daughter there and wants to reconnect with her."

"Okay, and tell me what your girlfriend is like?"

"Jackie? She's great! Very supportive and she has a great head on her shoulders...she's not a user, if that's what you're thinking."

"Okay, good. So, what happened today that upset you, Brad?"

"Well, I needed to find my passport and birth certificate today, since I might be moving to Ontario. So I asked my mom where they were. When I went to find them, I found a stack of letters addressed to me that I had never seen before. They were from my father!"

"Oh! Wow!" Michael knew Brad's background and understood how much this would affect him.

"Ya, he said how sorry he was and how much he missed me. I was so angry! I didn't understand why my mom would keep those letters from me over the years, so I confronted her and then left the house. I told Jackie that I had one more thing to do before we leave tonight, and headed to the prison to see Dad.

When I got there and started talking with him, I began to understand why Mom had such hard feelings when it came to him?"

"What did he say when he saw you, Brad?" Michael asked.

"He was happy to see me and he gave me a hug. Then he started to tell me that everything he did was for Mom and me. Even when I told him what happened after he was arrested, he still claimed that he did it all for us!" Brad was getting more and more upset, feeling as though he was starting to spin out of control. "I need something to help me calm down!"

"No, you don't, Brad. Just talk to me. Let's work through this. It's very understandable that you would be upset right now," Michael said in a calm voice. 'I think it would be a good idea for you to seek out a therapist once you get settled in Niagara Falls. The one-on-one counselling will be very helpful for you in this process. Remember, Brad, this is all a process. More and more emotions are going to come to the surface, but please remember how far you've come! You have done the right thing by calling me today. That shows me that you know that going back to drugs is not something that you really want in your life. Right?"

"Yes, you're right, Michael. I know that drugs aren't the answer. I also know that I will mess up my future with Jackie if I go back to them. I know that they won't solve my problems. But man, the temptation is hard to resist!"

"Yes, I know, Brad. I understand. Even after being twenty years clean, I still get the urge to use. I just have to remember why I quit. I reach out to *my* sponsor just like you have. Remember, Brad, it's okay to have feelings. And also remember that healing takes time. Be patient with yourself and don't put yourself down for having these weak moments. It's part of the process."

"Thanks, Michael. I think I'm going to be okay now. I really appreciate that you are always there for me!" Brad felt gratitude and hope...and strength.

"You're welcome, Brad. Now go and make good memories with Jackie! Look for a therapist in Niagara and please remember that I am always here to listen!" With that, Michael ended their conversation.

Brad sensed that Michael had helped him push past the urge he had been feeling. He returned to the car and checked the time: *9:30pm! Already?! Longer than I thought, but still enough time...thank goodness!*

When Brad arrived back at Jackie's, he found his mom, Jackie and her aunt Jane sitting there, visibly upset.

"Brad!" called his mom as he walked through the door. "I'm so sorry!"

"I know, Mom. I'm sorry, too. I went to see Dad. He's everything you said he was!"

Now Jackie was hugging him. She was so thankful he had come back in one piece.

"I wish you had let me read the letters when they came, Mom, but I do see now what you were trying to protect me from. He still doesn't get that what he did was wrong!"

"You're right, Honey. I don't think he ever will, unfortunately. Are you okay?"

"Ya. I really wanted to use again. It was the first in a long time that I felt like that.

"What did you do?" asked Jackie, wide-eyed.

"I called Michael, my sponsor. He reminded me how far I've come. He told me to make sure I find a therapist in Niagara Falls."

"Good for you, Brad!" All three very relieved, happy women shouted for joy.

"I love you so much, Honey, and I really hope this will be a great start for you!" said Brad's mother.

"I love you, too, Mom. I know it will be."

"I'll keep him in line!" Jackie teased.

Aunt Jane felt a twinge of fear in her gut for Jackie. She

really hoped that this would all

work out for them.

49

Tom woke up the next morning in a sterile prison cell. *Ugh! Why does my back hurt!* Every time he lifted his head, he had a pounding headache and felt sick. The worst part was, he was all alone. No one to yell at. No one. Completely alone.

"Oh, look! Sleeping beauty's awake!" said a deep male voice from outside his cell.

Tom tried to turn his head to see who it was, but it hurt too much. "Stop! Please, stop!" he replied in a whisper.

"What's the matter, Son? Does your head hurt? Huh? Feeling sick, maybe? You were a pretty big mess when they hauled you in here last night!" There was that voice again.

"Stop!" yelled Tom and held his head in pain.

"Well, Son, you are free to go," said the voice.

"Oh, did my mom finally show up?" Tom's impatience was obvious.

"Nope! No one is here, but I've enjoyed your company long enough!"

Tom finally managed to turn and see who was talking to him. He was a big scary looking prison guard, with arms the size of thighs. He had a buzz cut and he looked to be in his fifties. Not someone to mess with! This was the first time Tom was in a position that he couldn't control. He had never felt so lost, so alone, so scared.

"Well, how am I going to get home?" Tom asked.

"If you want, I can have an officer drive you home," replied the guard.

This is so humiliating, Tom thought. He couldn't believe that no one had shown up for him! Now he was starting to get angry. There was no way he was going to give anyone the satisfaction of seeing him being brought home by the police!

"Do you want a ride home or are you walking?" the guard yelled, perturbed by Tom's inaction.

"I'll walk." The prison was probably about an hour's walk away from his home.

"Okay, Son, I hope I don't see you in here again!" the guard replied.

"Ya." Tom walked out the door.

It was a bright, sunny day. Tom's head was pounding. He didn't even know what time it was, but he assumed it was early because the streets were mostly empty. At first he couldn't remember much from the night before, but as he walked, it started coming back to him. *Ugh!* he thought. *Why am I letting this get to me so much? Mom just doesn't care about me... at all! Robbie and Sarah showed up at the prom deliberately to make me mad. Who cares that Sarah and Robbie are together now? And Joanna... Joanna sure didn't stand by me! She doesn't know what she's missing!*

This was an all-time low for Tom. He felt defeated for the first time in his life. The truth was staring him right in the face but he couldn't accept it. It was obvious to him that he had some blame here, but it was too painful for him to admit that, even to himself. He quickly found ways to blame everyone else.

Tom tried to re-focus his thoughts, and started feeling better. But only a minute later, that gnawing feeling in his gut came back. *Man,* he thought, *I don't know what this feeling is!* The once confident, cocky Tom was now reduced to tears at the side of the road. He tried to stop the tears from coming, but they continued to flow. This was rock bottom. He didn't know what kind of reception he would get at home, but he realized that he had to apologize to his mom. *That's where I have to start! Mom!* That was the only thought that brought Tom some kind of peace as he continued to walk. He didn't know what he would say or where the words would come from—this was a scary new direction for him. This could mean that he would have to face a lot of other things he didn't like about himself. He didn't have any idea how to change, but somehow he knew

476

his mom would be able to point him in the right direction.

At home, Carole hadn't slept a wink all night. She had tossed and turned questioning her decision to leave Tom in jail. This went against her nature, but she just couldn't let him continue on this downward spiral. His dad had controlled their whole married life; she wasn't going to let her own son do the same. She was getting a backbone! Although she felt guilty, it felt really good!

Some of Carole's old friends had reached out to her

477

when Tom's dad died. They were starting to see the Carole they had missed all these years. Suddenly, she seemed to be coming alive again! She could leave the house and return whenever she pleased! It was wonderful!

The front door opened and that familiar surge of fear that Carole had felt for so many years started to rise in her. She quickly questioned everything she had just felt so good about seconds before. Her heart raced!

"Tom, is that you?" Her voice quivered.

"Ya, Mom, it's me," replied Tom.

Carole braced herself for that yelling that she was so used to having directed at her. She was ready for the demeaning words that had been slung at her more times than she could count. *I'm going to stand my ground this time*, she told herself. *He can't control me anymore!*

Tom came into the living room with tears streaming down his face.

479

"Tom, Honey! What's wrong?!" Carole's defenses dropped as he collapsed at her feet. He was physically and emotionally exhausted.

"Mom, I messed up," he cried. "I messed everything up! I'm sorry," he said over and over.

"It's okay, Tom. We'll get through this together." Carole was also in tears.

"No, it's not okay, Mom! I've treated you so bad all these years! I thought Dad was right. I thought that the way he treated you was okay—but it never was!

I'm so sorry, Mom! I'm sorry for all the trouble I've caused. Can you ever forgive me?" Tom looked pathetic—a grown man sobbing on the floor. But that didn't matter to Carole. Tom would always be her little boy.

"Yes, Tom! I forgive you, Honey! We can make a fresh start."

50

Prom had been a whirlwind of emotions for Sarah. She and Robbie had a great time together. They were excited for John and Rebecca, but they were also shaken to the core after Tom had made such a scene with Joanna. Sarah felt so bad for the humiliation Joanna had suffered, and she also thanked her lucky stars that it wasn't her—if she had not left Tom when she did, it would have been her! Sarah wondered what had happened to

Tom, but it didn't matter to her anymore, and that felt good. She appreciated Robbie even more now.

Sarah and Robbie had an amazing time at John and Rebecca's wedding. It seemed strange that she was watching someone else marry her best friend's ex-husband. *But that's life, isn't it? You can never know what the future may hold,* she mused.

Two years later, Robbie asked Sarah to marry him, and they were married that spring.

Sarah became more involved in her dad's carpentry business, which had grown to 20 employees over the years. They had more work than they knew what to do with. Sarah felt ready and confident to take over the business when her dad was ready to retire.

Robbie went to Bible College and fulfilled his dream of becoming a youth pastor and working with kids at their local church. Life was good, but Sarah still struggled with anxiety from her past. The relationship with

Tom had definitely left some scars. There were insecurities and negative thinking that she couldn't get over, as hard as she tried. She found herself second guessing her decisions, or keeping her head down when they were out. She was afraid of a backlash if she accidently looked at another man. Even though Robbie would never act like Tom, it didn't matter—Tom was still in her head. No matter how many times Robbie assured her everything was okay, she still felt uneasy.

Then there was Robbie's job. He worked closely with his team, some of whom were women. There were late nights and even some weekends away with the youth. Sarah would go once in a while, but her job wouldn't let her get away very often. Logically, Sarah knew she could trust Robbie, but every time he left the house, she wondered. Would this be the day she'd catch him doing something like Tom? It didn't matter that it had been years before when that had happened to her—the wounds were still there and they were still deep. She would see the way the women at church would look at Robbie, and the way they would run to his side to talk with him about future events or about their own children. She realized that anxiety could make everything seem suspicious and everyone seem guilty.

Although Sarah tried not to let bad memories get the better of her, she and Robbie would often end up having heated discussions about it. Finally one day, she decided that she needed help dealing with this and sought help from a therapist. Robbie supported her completely. She discovered that the problem was more than just issues with Tom. Jackie's leaving had left a big hole in her life. She knew that she missed her best friend, but she didn't realize how much it had affected her. They had always spent so much time together— they had been soulmates. Then, all of a sudden, Jackie had left without warning. Even though they could talk on the phone once in a while, it wasn't the same. Jackie would talk about the new people she had met; Sarah would find herself feeling slighted and jealous. As she worked through all these emotions with her therapist she finally began to feel some peace. Gradually, she was able to let her guard down with Robbie and accept that Jackie had a new life out in Vancouver.

Then news of Jackie's mom changed everything.

51

Jackie and Brad left
Vancouver on Sunday night and
arrived in Niagara Falls early
Monday morning. There were a
few new Tim Horton's donut
shops in the area and new
shopping plazas here and there.
All of a sudden, the feelings she
had run away from came
flooding back—the feelings of
being overwhelmed and
misunderstood; the feelings of
anger that she had never dealt
with. Tears stung her eyes as

Jackie and Brad made their way to her mom's—now her—house. As they walked in, it all looked the same. It still had the smell of stale smoke and booze. It was all too much for Jackie. Suddenly, she felt as if she was suffocating! She ran outside and tried to calm herself. Brad followed her. He had a deep understanding of what was happening to her—he had felt that way many times after his dad was taken away.

Once Jackie felt a bit more composed, she went inside again

and came face-to-face with her mom's coffee cup, still sitting on the counter. And there was her mom's blanket still on the couch. It was like nothing had changed even though everything had. She walked up to her old room and saw that her mom hadn't changed a thing in it except that there was now a crib set up for those times she babysat Abigail. Jackie was glad that John had still let her mom be a part of Abigail's life after all that had happened. *Once the funeral is over,* Jackie thought, *I'm going to*

try to rebuild my relationship with
Abigail.

Jackie's Aunt Jane flew in later that night after she had tied up some loose ends with her work. She had offered to pay for whatever kind of funeral Jackie would want to give her mom, as there was no other money for it. Jackie decided an intimate graveside ceremony would be perfect, then maybe a small reception at a local church. They made the arrangements for the following Friday. There was no other family except Jackie and

Aunt Jane, but there would be friends and co-workers coming to pay their respects. Jackie needed to call Sarah.

Jackie and Sarah hadn't spoken nearly enough over the last couple of years since she left. It wasn't that she didn't want to talk to Sarah, and it definitely wasn't that she didn't miss her, it was just that talking with her brought up everything she had run away from. Every time they talked, John and Abigail would inevitably come up in the conversation and it became very clear that Sarah and John kept in touch a lot. Jackie knew that she had no right to be upset, but at the same time she almost felt like Sarah was a friend of the enemy. Sarah hadn't invited Jackie to her wedding a couple years ago. It hurt Jackie a lot, but she knew that John would have been there and it would have been awkward for all involved. Outwardly, it would have seemed that John hadn't done anything wrong in his relationship with Jackie. He was a wonderful, supportive father and he had wanted to be a good husband, but Jackie resented the guilt and pressure he had put her under regarding Abigail. The last time she spoke with Sarah, Sarah had mentioned something about John getting married. For some reason, a surge of jealousy had flooded over her. That surprised her because she knew that it was she who had walked away from him. What had she expected him to do?

"Hello?"

"Hey, Sarah. It's me, Jackie."

"Hey, Jackie! How are you?"

"I'm okay."

"I was planning to call you this morning. I'm so sorry to hear about your mom, Jackie! We miss her already. She meant so much to all of us."

"Thanks, Sarah. It was a shock, for sure. We just got in last night." Jackie replied.

"We?"

"Yes. Brad and Aunt Jane came with me."

"Oh! I finally get to meet Brad." Sarah tried to sound excited.

Jackie could feel the forced effort, but she didn't acknowledge it. There was too much water under the bridge. Jackie decided not to mention her thoughts about Abigail— that would be a conversation for another time.

The next few days were busy preparing for Barb's funeral and getting through it. Brad was Jackie's rock the whole time. He was strong for both her and Aunt Jane. Jackie wondered if John would show up at the funeral and if he might bring Abigail with him.

She was so young.

52

John sat in the kitchen, deep in thought, and white as a sheet. Rebecca found him there and was instantly concerned.

"John? Are you okay? Who was on the phone?"

"It was Jackie. Her mom died!" John replied.

"Barb? Oh no! So, Barb didn't survive the accident! How horrible! Horrible and sad!" They sat in stunned silence for a few moments. "We're going to miss her, John...and so will Abigail."

"I know. It's so sad. Jackie's coming back to the Falls to arrange for the funeral and everything. And...uh...Rebecca...she also said that she wants to be in Abigail's life now!" They looked at each other, wordless. "You're Abigail's mother now, Rebecca! Jackie left! I don't want you to ever question that, okay?"

Rebecca didn't feel reassured, but she replied, "I know, John. I love you."

Jackie's return was something that John and Rebecca had not yet discussed, but for each of them it often had played in the back of their minds. John realized that they needed to talk with a lawyer just to learn about their rights, and decided to do that right away. This could be their worst nightmare.

Then, there was the matter of the funeral. Since Abigail was close to Barb, should they take her to the funeral? Was she too young? Would they be wrong if they didn't take her? They struggled with what that all could

mean for their little family. They

felt so torn that they decided to

get some advice from their

pastor. He told them that there

was no right or wrong answer

about bringing Abigail. He

advised them to pray about it and

do what they felt would bring the

most peace. Regarding Jackie's

return, he said that since she was

Abigail's biological mother, and

as long as there were clear

boundaries and safe, loving

relationships, it didn't need to be

a problem. They decided to take

Abigail to the funeral even though

she wouldn't really understand what was happening.

Seeing Jackie again was strange for John. He now realized that—over the years after she left—he had dealt with most of his emotions about that, and the fact that Jackie had left didn't need to matter now. He felt that he owed it to Abigail to give her time with Jackie. Abigail didn't remember Jackie, so visits were short at first. Jackie would take her to the park for an hour, and John or Rebecca would be near, on standby. This went on for a couple months.

Jackie had found it very difficult to see John again. But she was thankful that he and Rebecca were so open to her being around Abigail. Rebecca was a great communicator and she never seemed to judge Jackie. John and Rebecca actually seemed to have accepted her into their lives. Things weren't always smooth and easy, but they all tried their best.

53

Over the next few months, Jackie and Brad started to make the house their own. Aunt Jane had generously given them some money, both to deal with the mortgage that was still owing on the house and to tie them over until they each found jobs.

Brad started submitting resumes to local garages looking for mechanics, but he didn't have much work experience as a mechanic, so the search continued. One day an ad appeared in the newspaper: a local shop owner was looking for a mechanic to maintain their service vehicles.

"Hey, Jackie," Brad called toward the kitchen. "Isn't this Sarah's family's shop?

"Yes, it is...." Jackie read the ad, a bit apprehensive. She didn't know what kind of reception Brad would get if he applied. But, at the same time, she knew that if anyone would take a chance on someone who needed a second chance like Brad, it would be

Sarah's parents. "Go for it, Babe!" she finally said. "I think you should apply!"

Jackie thought it might be better if Brad simply applied, rather than her calling Sarah. She was afraid that Sarah would think she was only calling her for a favour. Even though she missed Sarah, she knew that this was the best way to deal with this situation.

The next day, Brad went to the Sanders' shop. He still hadn't met Sarah or her family, so they wouldn't know his connection with

Jackie. The ad had said to ask for Greg. When Brad arrived at the shop he saw a very busy operation. He walked in and was met by a lady at the counter. *That must be Sarah's mom*, he thought.

"Good morning, how can I help you?" Jen asked with a smile.

"Good morning. I'm here to apply for the mechanic job."

'Okay, great! You just might be the answer to our prayers! I'll go and find Greg for you!"

"Thank you so much!" replied Brad, feeling a certain warmth that he had never felt before. He could see why Jackie spoke so highly of them.

"Good day, Sir! It's nice to meet you. I'm Greg." He reached to shake Brad's hand. There was an unassuming kindness in Greg's eyes. Brad felt at ease talking to him. Any nervousness he had, melted away in that moment.

"Hello, Greg. It's really nice to meet you, too. I'm Brad

Hutchins. I'm very interested in your mechanic's job!"

"Do you have any schooling to back you up?" Greg asked.

"Yes, I do. It's all in here," Brad said as he handed Greg his resume.

Greg read it over carefully, frequently asking questions, then nodded.

"You came here all the way from Vancouver?" asked Greg, surprised.

"Yes, I came here with my girlfriend after her mother died." Brad wasn't sure if Greg would put two and two together.

"I'm sorry about your loss." Then, after a moment, Greg raised the resume, flashed a knowing smile at Brad, and said, "Looks good to me, Son. When can you start?"

"As soon as you want me!" Brad couldn't hide his excitement.

"Tomorrow, 8:00 a.m. Oh, and give my love to Jackie!" With a twinkle in his eye, and a smile on his face, Greg turned and walked away to continue his work.

"Sounds good. Thank you! And, I will!" said Brad with a laugh. *What a cool guy,* he thought.

54

Tom was in therapy for a long time. It took years to fix what his father had broken in him. He married a very kind and loving woman. They had 4 children and his mother moved in with them to help with the children.

Tom went to both Joanna and Sarah and apologized for how he had treated them in the past. Both women had a hard time accepting the apology, but they did and were eventually able to forgive him. Sarah and Tom would cross paths once in a while

and they'd smile and wave but

continue on. For each of them, to

be able to do that was progress!

55

Brad and Jackie were excited and grateful that Greg had hired him. Jackie couldn't help but wonder how Sarah would feel about Jackie's boyfriend working for her dad. She hoped it would all work out.

Brad arrived at the shop the next morning, half an hour early, excited and ready to start his new job. As he walked into the shop, he was met by a woman about his age.

"Good morning, I'm Sarah," Sarah reached out to shake his hand.

"Good morning, Sarah, I'm Brad." Brad felt apprehensive about how he would be received by Sarah. He wondered if her father had told her yet who he was.

"I know who you are, Brad," she replied. "Welcome to the team."

"Thank you, Sarah." He felt a bit unsure what to think of that welcome. He was then whisked away by an impressed Greg to

start working on one of their
trucks.

Sarah's parents had filled
her in on the fact that Brad was
going to be working for them. She
had wrestled with all the emotions
she felt over Jackie leaving the
way she did. She hadn't sleep
much that night, but she came to
a very important conclusion.

'Hey, Brad", said Sarah.

"Yes?" Brad was on high
alert, trying not to mess anything
up.

"Is Jackie home?"

"Yes, she is," replied Brad with a smile on his face.

"Hey, Dad, do you mind if I take off for a while?"

"Take all the time you need, Honey"

It was time to make amends with her best friend. Jackie and Sarah spent the whole day hashing out everything that had come between them. The anger and tears eventually turned into laughter and hugs. They both decided that life was too short to not be with the people that you care about!

56

Brad excelled at the shop. Both Brad and Jackie became very close with Sarah, Robbie and the rest of Sarah's family. They were there when Sarah and Robbie welcomed their children—a boy and a girl—and Sarah was there to help Jackie navigate her own life as a mother.

Abigail was loved very much by her unique family. As time went on, John and Rebecca were able to become friends with

Jackie and Brad. There was no more animosity between them— just their common love for a beautiful little girl. They split their time with her and celebrated holidays together so none of them would miss the important times with her.

Jackie and Brad were married soon after Brad started working for Sarah's family. They loved their life. Greg and Brad worked together on the renovation of Jackie's house.

Jackie's priorities changed from wanting to be a successful

career woman to wanting more children and staying at home with them. In the years that followed they became foster parents and Sarah, Robbie, John, and Rebecca—all of whom shared the same passion—helped out with the children. Sarah's company eventually built an addition onto Jackie's house that they developed into a drop-in youth ministry...and they all shared a part in running it. When Abigail got older, she helped, too!

None of them thought their lives would end up the way they

did. The twists and turns; the losses and gains. At the end of the day, though, they were all happy. What else could one ask for?

57

One day, years later, on a crisp September morning, Sarah and Jackie sat on the balcony of their seniors' apartment—both in their nineties now, and both widows.

They each sat with a cup of tea in hand and laughed at the memories from their childhood and high school—the way Sarah was so boy crazy and Jackie was so career-focussed. They were now able to laugh at the irony of Jackie being the one who got pregnant way back then. They shuddered at the memories that were hard to relive. Pain still filled Jackie's eyes when she remembered leaving Abigail for all that time. She was so thankful that Abigail had forgiven her. They were both teary over the length of time that they had grown apart, and over Brad's illness and passing, and then Robbie's. They had been each other's rock through so much of their lives. They had both attended the weddings of their children, and had welcomed grandchildren together.

Sarah was thankful that her friendship with Jackie had withstood the test of time, even though they had lost their way for a while. She looked over at her best friend—no longer the picture of youth—and was filled with gratitude that they had had the privilege of growing old together.

Amber hopes you have enjoyed this book, and the hope is that you will be on the look out for upcoming books by Amber. Her passion and new ideas for more books grows each day, and she is exploring a few ideas to keep you coming back to read more.

Made in the USA
Monee, IL
24 November 2020

49445127R00308